The Department
of Missing Persons

THE DEPARTMENT OF MISSING PERSONS

A Novel

Ruth Zylberman

*Translated from the French
by Grace McQuillan*

Arcade Publishing • New York

First English-language edition

First published in France in 2015 under the title *La direction de l'absent* by
Christian Bourgois Editeur

This is a work of fiction. Names, characters, places, and incidents are either the
products of the author's imagination or used fictitiously.

Arcade Publishing books may be purchased in bulk at special discounts for sales
promotion, corporate gifts, fund-raising, or educational purposes. Special edi-
tions can also be created to specifications. For details, contact the Special Sales
Department, Arcade Publishing, 307 West 36th Street, 11th Floor, New York,
NY 10018 or arcade@skyhorsepublishing.com.

Arcade Publishing® is a registered trademark of Skyhorse Publishing, Inc.®,
a Delaware corporation.

Visit our website at www.arcadepub.com.

10 9 8 7 6 5 4 3 2 1

Library of Congress Cataloging-in-Publication Data is available on file.

Cover design by Brian Peterson

Print ISBN: 978-1-62872-803-3
Ebook ISBN: 978-1-62872-806-4

Printed in the United States of America

PART I

The State of Things

1

—◆—

And the city stood in its brightness.
And the city stood in its brightness when years later I returned.
Czesław Miłosz
(Translated by the poet and Robert Hass, 1963)

WHEN MY MOTHER REALIZED I wanted to die, at the time I was a woman between two ages, she became frightened. Until then I had been a good little *bijou* who was very much alive, but I was almost forty years old and I wanted to die.

I had to look under the green liquid mass; I had to look under the sludge and sink down, body outstretched, and absorb the water. Let my tangled hair hang over my shoulders, let my tangled hair hang over my eyes and face. Get used to the mass of hair, get used to the mass of water. Let myself soak, envelop, and leave on tiptoe for the water's end, toward its down-below. Travel through the water without flapping my arms or legs. Accept the coughing and spitting and the cold everywhere along my body. I looked around me at the surface of the water, the bits of floating wood, and the lacy shrubs and bushes on the surrounding banks. On the other side, all the way up the hill and at regular intervals, the trees soared upward with every inch of their trunks. Their black branches, immaculate, stretched toward the sky. They were a woeful army of comrades.

They were cold, cold, cold. I was cold, and I felt my feet going numb in the water. The world was deserted. All my faces had disappeared behind the tracery of trunks and branches. They were sunken, swallowed up, and my body was no longer inside my body. It had become a naked tree, a branch. The hills and trails were swallowed up with every-thing else around my living body, the one that walked in step, at a trot, or at a gallop to the beat of my heart and the blood pounding in my head. From my side of the water, I saw it in front of me: the sweep of naked trees, the sorrowful army of comrades. It, that, I shiver against the branches raised to the sky and the earth all around and the fragile expanse of water. I, that, it moves to the middle of the water.

The sound of silence: my long breath mixed with the wind.

I remembered hills and trails, the hardness of the sun, dreamed faces that floated superimposed on the dazzling green of meadows, brown ridges of cut lavender on the hillside, the lone horse that had turned its head to watch me pass. I remembered the gray building façades in Paris and my eyes glued to the rows of balustrades. Everything had to be numbed, and the suffering reduced to silence, in the cold water and the naked trees. I just had to let myself drift to the middle of the water, between the two banks. It was time for my own death. It was time, unavoidable at last, for my own death.

I dragged the traces of crossed centuries with me to the bottom of the water, the traces of the werewolf century I'd tried so hard to keep alive, as my mother had done before me. I had been her eternal life, her miracle, unaffected by fog and gray lands. Unharmed. An escaped bird she sent out to conquer the wide world.

And the world began with Paris. *Maman* knew all the streets and shortcuts; she held me by the hand. It was 1978. In the 18th arrondissement, she was in her own kingdom; black curls, high cheekbones, and shining eyes, paying no attention to the men turning their heads in her direction. The Algerians of Barbès-Rochechouart mistook her for one of their own, and would murmur in Arabic when she passed. They had no idea that, for her, the desert dated back thousands of years, and between the desert and Barbès there had been a detour through the austere plains of Poland.

We'd get off at la Goutte-d'Or: condemned buildings with windows sealed off by wooden beams set in the shape of a cross, people sitting on sidewalks, the muffled cries of a brawl, the soft steps of African women. It was like the city border, the continental border, even. I crossed over the edge and descended the hills, my hand in my mother's. She'd have long conversations in a low voice with a butcher who had known her father during the war, and whose shop on rue Myrha was surrounded by the gaping holes of demolition: no man's lands, pits, and sand. I noticed everything and sensed the mystery of the city in decay, the almost invisible movement of time attacking the fronts of the buildings . . .

Maman would emerge from between the ruins and I'd take the lead, running several feet ahead just so I could turn around and rush back to her. Hand in hand, we took rue Doudeauville and made our way to the top of the neighborhood in no time at all. We circled around la Butte following the curve of rue Caulaincourt, sheltered by the leaves of trees planted evenly on both sides of the street. Reunited in the center, their branches looked like a botanical dais.

Here, and for me it was the heart of Paris, the houses were built straight up and down and made of brick and plaster, eternal. All the movements of the street—the comings and goings of passersby, the noise of cars, the alternating darkness and light at nightfall, when the apartment windows behind the façades would light up and then go out—were accidents. Their anecdotal and uncertain matter dissolved in that landscape of stone where Maman paved the way for me. When she walked, as I observed looking up at her, she often wore a slight smile that seemed intended for invisible presences only she could detect. She led me down a narrow street bordering the gardens of the Sacré-Cœur. When I ventured there alone, I was always frightened by the little caves dug into the rock, vestiges of the Montmartre gypsum mines. A barely legible plaque announced that Cuvier had discovered fossilized bones here in 1798. Nothing, however, announced that at the same location, less than a century later, Communards had been executed and the hollowed-out pits used to bury their bodies.

I knew nothing about the Paris Commune, but—did I have some kind of intuition about the massacre?—I was certain that those stony, dark, and stinking pits harbored troubling spirits that my mother put to flight with only the force of her absentminded smile.

She dressed me, she made me read, and she contemplated me. From my bedroom door I'd feel her eyes resting on me, checking under the colorful dresses she bought me incessantly for the uninterrupted flow of aliveness. Without touching me, she listened to the regular beating of my heart and measured the path of blood in my body, the filling of my veins. She also saw the words in books and images as they inscribed themselves inside my head. To be wise, studious, and polite; I knew very well that wasn't what was most important. The command my mother silently threw to me from the doorway, the marvelous project in which she obliged me to take part, *that* was most important: to grow . . . my skin nice and warm, my eyes bright.

In truth, it wasn't a difficult task: let my blood circulate, breathe, let my heart beat, and at last grow up. There was nothing I had to do except let myself go, and let her hopeful gaze take root in me like a plant irrigated by water.

That was my entire childhood: my mother's beauty and the city she transformed. On the bus, she lifted me onto her lap and I watched Paris pass by. The solid city, made of evenly measured cut stone, was the mineral and welcoming double of my mother's abundant body, a body-shelter I had occasionally seen naked. Stripped of its erotic fluctuations, it was like a veiny block, granular but unassailable. Sitting on my mother's lap, her arms around my body, I felt her chest against my back. The bus rushed over the Seine and I fell into a deep sleep against her, a sleep like that of an animal or an infant. I heard the distant sound of passengers, the muffled noise of tires and brakes on the pavement. I didn't worry about missing part of the trip, though, because *that* trip, in that city handed to me like a gift, was one I believed I would be led to take many more times, an incalculable number of times, maybe even forever: the infinite length of time that my infinite childhood beside Maman would last.

And so we went, pressed together, over the white sand paths of the Jardin du Luxembourg, where the life both of us wished for was possible: one that was self-sustaining and established on the unsinkable foundations of peace and joy.

And when she pushed me on the green swings to go as high as the tops of the trees, in my own delight I carried the breath of her joy. All the way to the jagged sky between the branches, I brought her prayers for immortality.

My mother's face. To be studied closely, even when she's sleeping. I came close to the bed. It was dawn. A halo of white light unveiled her cheeks, the path of wrinkles, the still new corruption of her skin. I scrutinized each part. I try to determine where the power comes from, the radiance, and I leaned over her the way one leans over a reflection. I recognized the tip of the vein that beats under the skin at the top of her neck. The line of her eyebrows and the triangle of her face. Skin that vibrates. My mother's face, an abrupt shield on which I searched for the geological traces of the child she was, the child who escaped the snow and cold—a long time ago, in the snow, the stuff of legends—pulled by her mother's arm. I knew it, I always knew it, without even needing to be told. I looked at her again. My mother, whose face in its childhood proportions touched the deadly snow and bodies piled on top of each other. It was during the war, and the face that should have never grown old but remained always that of a dead child, buried under snow with her head turned beneath the pile of corpses, that face was saved by her mother out, out, out—tremendous strength was required—from under the snow. The face becomes distorted under the imprint of an image that chills me, and I recoiled in fear because through her forehead, far behind the roots of her hair, inside my mother's head, among the cells, in the midst of the living magma, I saw a tree growing with branches encircling a vast white expanse. And from that landscape, I knew this too, one cannot run away. But Maman opened her eyes and the face recomposed itself; invincible, back from the dead.

For me and for herself, she sought out the landscapes of her rebirth. She brought me to a hidden area east of the Rhône in the south of France. We passed through villages. The road, at first flat and straight, rose up after a bend uncovering a jumble of open, gently sloping pastures. Another village; a temple, a church in the center, houses with tiled roofs grouped above the coursing of a river. We kept going.

Then, as if to escape the world, a small road on the left. First we couldn't see anything, just a few trees along the path. Then came the dark and evenly cut rectangles of the lavender fields. Finally, one by one, and each of these appearances was like a greeting, came the round hills that looked like a group of sisters, calm and laughing.

We took to the trails, rocks mixed with earth, our souls on alert: the blue and mauve patches of flowers, the harshness of the wind, the rustling of the grasses, the empty river bed, and the trees that turned green in uneven tufts of wet and shiny leaves. It was the necessary thread of growth and decline and growth again, renewed indefinitely. Below the hills it finally seemed possible to settle on the ground, to really stay, with our skin and coats like mended scraps on the fields of cut wheat, and to take shelter from the world's brutality.

In a drawer in my room, I kept the photo strips she took me to get in the booth at the Blanche *métro* station. For the background, you could choose the Sacré-Cœur or the Moulin Rouge. She chose the Sacré-Cœur. I climbed onto her lap, we set the shutter, and we waited for the flash. We spent the three minutes while the film developed in silence, dancing from one foot to another in the cold air of the *métro*. The photos came out of the machine, always identical: softened by the same orange filter, my face out of the frame and my head turned, looking at Maman who smiled without moving, looking right at the flash.

Year after year, the composition never changed. The Sacré-Cœur behind us was an extension of ourselves, our symbolic home, and an assurance that we inhabited this place the same way it inhabited us.

Year after year, photo after photo, my childhood went by: a mass of hours and actions governed by routine and repetition, indistinct hours stuck to one another with the saliva of kisses, the friction of caresses, and the white secretions of tears. And, like a precious flower under the artificial sun of a greenhouse, while I went to school and out to the yard and to piano lessons, while I read in my bedroom and ate dinner at night in the kitchen with my parents, while I went to the Grand Palais every Sunday morning with Father where we admired its sparkling glass shell and the clouds reflected in it, while I resisted the cruelty of children at school and was cruel to them in turn, while I looked at adults and city streets like movie extras on a sleeping set, like a precious flower under the artificial sun of a greenhouse, my soul and heart were polished in anticipation of life and love.

Night was coming, and the silent languages were coming to power.

First, there was only a map: no buildings or sidewalks, just a drawing of the streets and their familiar names I flew over without thinking, like a luminous and naive soul returning serenely to her birthplace. I flew above the little ghetto, rue Sienna, rue Pańska, then I took off to the north, rue Miła, right onto Zamenhof, Gęsia on the right, Nalewki and Place Muranowski on the left. Familiar too was the passenger bridge on rue Chłodna with the wobbly tramway underneath. My list of addresses: 13 rue Leszno, 17 rue Krochmalna, 27 rue Nowolipki, 26 rue Grzybowska, 16 rue Leszno, 19 rue Zamenhof, 18 rue Miła, 22 rue Franciszkańska, 32 rue Elektoralna.

It's the enclave of my dreams, hemmed in by high walls. I see only the map, the names of streets I fly over without thinking. The faces and silhouettes are invisible, or rather I only glimpse them, recognizing a few: the pianist, the little smugglers, the singer, the beggar children, the distraught mothers, the cannibalistic mothers. I don't look closely, though; I'm too afraid. Their eyes, the lice, and their terror fill *me* with terror, so I fly and fly. I see only the map, the names of streets I fly over without thinking. To avoid Karmelicka, I learn the secret passages between rue Nowolipki and rue Leszno.

I am the soul of life returned from pacified times.

And in reality, *I* am the ghost among the panic-stricken Jews who walk and die between rue Niska and Muranowska. A ghost from the future, bullet-proof, fear-proof, untouchable. Except that I lose my way, I linger over the sidewalks, next to the walls, near the bunkers that no longer exist, and under the paving stones. Alone and horrified, in the nights of my post-war, I hear noises under the earth's crust, those of molten bodies that keep exploding. And I don't remember these sounds; I am the only one who hears them.

"Maman." I'd yell loud enough for her to hear me at the other end of the hallway. She came.

2

———◆———

I WAS BORN IN the 10th arrondissement in Paris on April 30, 1971. In other words, twenty-six years after the end of the War, the only one that counts, the second one. For a long time I thought twenty-six years was a lot. More precisely, I believed for a long time that I'd been born in another space-time—after a sort of new Big Bang, in a new universe, the fabulous world of "post-war"—and that as the chosen child, I was out of harm's way.

So let me rephrase. I was born on April 30 in the Year of Grace 26: splendidly alive, marvelously uncontaminated.

Twenty-six years; is that a little or a lot?

3

———◆———

FROM THE END OF the dark hallway, my mother would
come. What did I have to be afraid of? The great sorrows
were behind us. This was France in the eighties. Every morning I'd leave for school on rue de Clignancourt and regain
my peace of mind. The ground was stable under my feet.

France was not an abstraction. It had the firmness of the
engraved stone on the school building's pediment, the austere solemnity of the motto "Liberty, Equality, Fraternity,"
toward which I complicitly lifted my head before going
through the doors each day. It had the radiance of the tricolor flag and the unbending gentleness of Marianne's blind
eyes, seen from her perch on a pedestal among children's
drawings hanging on the wall. France had the clear sonority
of the old songs we copied into our notebooks; it was the

tidy parks of Île-de-France, the joyful abundance of Prisunic grocery stores, the unchanging loftiness of Racine's plays.

I used to rejoice on election days when the school was transformed into a polling station: in this blending of functions was the implicit affirmation of a continuity between the schoolchild and the voter, the certainty of an inescapably delineated way of life that would unfold within the schoolyard's four walls. The ballots lined up in piles on the table, the way everyone picked them up one by one to conceal whichever slip would eventually be slid into the envelope, the voting booths surrounded by a gray curtain where both my parents—with a conspiratorial air—would go in turn, the seriousness of the assessor who called out the names and addresses in a loud voice, the wonderful cry, "*A voté!*" underscoring the dropping of ballots into the box. These things were props on the set of "Democracy, Liberty, Frenchness" that filled me with joy. The tie my father put on for those occasions further strengthened my feeling that a true mystical communion was taking place: this was the public demonstration of our assimilation, the poignant advent of our identity as citizens. In that magnificent ritual I saw, vaguely, the necessary outcome of centuries in exile.

The certainty that we'd arrived safe and sound was reinforced further still whenever we visited my father's aunt, who lived in a small building on rue Daguerre two steps from the Lion de Belfort.

She had once been a knitting worker in the 11th arrondissement fur workshops, and after retiring, she'd reinvented herself as an amateur painter. Her exuberantly colored paintings depicted overabundant families captured inside crimson interiors: the women, with almond eyes and long black hair, wore turquoise dresses, the men had beards and multicolored caftans, and children with dark skin looked at the adults with trusting eyes. The aunt piled up her canvases in every corner of her apartment, cramming them against one another, in the kitchen, on the landing.

What was most fascinating was the way that Anna— who still wore her hair, now gray, the way she had when she was young, in two coils separated from one another by a part on top of her head—had painted the tiles in her apartment the same tawny colors she used for her paintings. Transformed into stained glass, the windows filtered a soft blue, yellow, and red-colored light into the rooms which, especially in summer, enveloped the furniture and the books piled on the library shelves in a surreal halo.

In one corner of the living room was a portrait of Anna at twenty years old. It was easy to see from her melancholy dark-haired gypsy gaze, her half-smile, her parted hair up in a chignon, and her long and shiny earrings, that the women with large eyes in her paintings were only an uninterrupted series of self-portraits.

The creator of the painting was a certain Schoenberg, Anna's great love before the war.

He had painted her face from memory, at the camp in Pithiviers where he'd been interned in 1941. Schoenberg, a tall and frail young man—judging by the only remaining photo of him, which was set on the speckled marble above the fireplace—had prefaced the drawing with a dedication: "To my beloved Chanouchi." He'd also drawn a staff, on which were reproduced the first notes of a Chopin nocturne that I tried in vain to decipher each time I visited.

There was also another "œuvre" by Schoenberg, a letter opener made of light wood on which he'd carved drawings of the barracks in Pithiviers with, once again, a music staff, but this time with the first notes of a Beethoven symphony. On the handle of the letter opener were written the following words, the irony or sadness of which I didn't consider at the time: "Fond memories of Pithiviers."

Anna would whistle me the nocturne, the beginning of the symphony, and then she would talk about Schoenberg, that boy who was so fragile, so artistic, so in love. For me, though, Schoenberg and his thin face in metal-rimmed glasses was just one more silhouette like the ones in the photos that populated my grandmothers' shelves. Faces of men, of women, of children, brothers, fathers, sisters, mothers, nephews, or nieces who had most likely existed at one time, somewhere, in places of which I'd glimpsed a few details: the thin bank of a river, the finely crafted walls of a wooden house, the gate of a railway station in the countryside.

This crowd of black and white—or rather white and gray, in which I sometimes saw a face strangely resembling one of my grandmothers or Parisian cousins, like a plant from the same species—was the crowd of the disappeared. These disappearances did not surprise me. "They died during the war." I'd gotten used to hearing that without asking questions long ago.

It seemed completely natural to me that Schoenberg, too, had disappeared, and that there were no traces left of him but those musical staffs, the portrait, and the letter opener.

Anna had also inherited one other thing from Schoenberg: his best friend, who came from the same village in Poland, who "didn't die in the war," and whom she'd married in the early fifties.

This was Morgenstern, the diabolical figure of rue Daguerre! Morgenstern—not much more than five feet tall, a few sparse teeth—who insisted, whenever he emerged from his library where books were piled from the parquet floor to the ceiling, on speaking to me in English (he'd learned it on his own by reading Shakespeare) because, he said, there was nothing more important than knowing other languages. He had a good grasp of ten or so, which completely baffled me, because if my English was rudimentary, then his—like his French, in fact—was scarcely comprehensible due to the combined effect of his accent and the absence of teeth.

But Morgenstern hardly worried about material details as trivial as teeth and accents. He would plant me in his old chair, brown leather with curved armrests, and give me, in English, the detailed inventory of his library:

"French Literature, Russian Literature, American Literature, English Literature." He'd point out each consecutive section with the hand gestures of a magician, haphazardly accentuating the syllables in each word. "*LittéraTUre française, LIittérature rrrrusse, LittéraToure aMMéricaine, Littérature anglaise* and then Polish Literature, Yiddish Literature, Spanish Literature, Italian, North European and now and now see, listen! BAUdelaire, Tsvetaïeva, Louise Labbé, Dostoïevski, KAfKA, Sade, John Donne, Knut KNUt Hamsun, WITKACY." He turned around. "*Philosophie*, Political SCIENCE, *Économie politique*, Trotski, Marx, Stuart Mill, Rousseau, Hegel, Platon. Nothing, nothing that is human is alien to me."

He'd pirouette from the window to the door, run his hand over the shelves, caress the bookbindings, blow on the dust-covered pages, and adjust the heaps.

"This book"—he took down from the shelves the theoretical texts of Rosa Luxembourg—"I bought on boulevard Saint-Michel, it was 1932, I had just arrived in Paris, East Railway Station, *gare de l'Est*, such an awful racket, I ran straight to the Latin Quarter, that's where I had been told to go, back there in Ostrow, Mazovie, Poland. In 1933, I also bought the first translation of Kafka, I could read in German of course but thought it could be interesting in French too. Just to compare, what do you think, little girl? *Dites-moi, jeune fille, et vous que lisez-vous*, WHAT DO YOU READ? What do Parisian little girl read?"

I didn't answer; I hadn't understood a thing! He found me a bit simple-minded, Morgenstern, but he'd put on a show for me because as far as spectators went, he didn't have very many. He lived cloistered on rue Daguerre, reading and rereading in his worn-out armchair. At his feet he had several wobbly stacks of books onto which he'd unthinkingly toss each volume that he'd finished. Certain ones had collapsed but he paid no attention, and the nation of books, creeping plank by plank, invaded each corner of the room like an unmanageable grass a little more every day.

Sometimes he'd bring me with him for a tour of the cemetery at Montparnasse. He'd shout at the dead, climb over the graves, and laughingly comment on the epitaphs. I walked ten steps behind him, certain that these sacrileges would not go unpunished. He found all of it beautiful and outrageous, these cemeteries surrounded by walls, with neatly traced paths where the dead lay quietly awaiting visits from the living. "Can you appreciate this: walls, paths, graves, how beautiful this is? Parisian girl!"

Once in a while, worried, Anna would suddenly open the door to the library, her hands blue with paint, and interrupt Morgenstern's tirades; she forbade him from bringing me to the cemetery.

She mixed French and Yiddish. He'd answer with dignity in English. "I try to give this Parisian little girl a sense of what aaaart and more specifically literatoure is. I don't know what she should be effrayeeed of."

21

She'd yell in Yiddish, her long gypsy earrings swinging in every direction, then take me out of the library and repatriate me to the "Schoenberg area" in the living room, force-feed me her cinnamon apple tart, white and brown, and let me play with the letter opener from Pithiviers. Then on her easel she'd continue her psychedelic explorations of squandered family happiness.

I interpreted this whole strange atmosphere as a collection of relics, the exoticism of which—from atop my pedestal as a schoolgirl fed with the peremptory slogans of the Republic—I could appreciate. They were the stages, emigration, deaths, accents, and follies that had been necessary in the end to lead to this perfection that was my French childhood in a world at peace. And rue Daguerre was, in essence, no more than a small lost island, an isolated embassy from "the world before" whose customs were not unpleasant to observe, and whose magic lights did perhaps capture the imagination, but then vanished immediately once across the Seine, where one's feet were replanted in the present.

On the other side of the Seine, in "the world of today"—impermeable to old troubles, the world of my blissful childhood—a new president of the Republic was elected, a socialist, and people danced in place de la Bastille to celebrate the coming of a new era. My parents did not share this surge of enthusiasm; they would have been too afraid of being noticed. It also would have required too much hope (the betterment of humankind!). They had lowered their ambitions immediately: it was enough just to carry on. It was in fact on this pessimistic conviction that their alliance rested, but I for my part enjoyed the scenes of rejoicing I saw on television.

Girls in tee-shirts brandished tricolor flags, perched on shoulders in the crowd. It was an updated revival of our history lessons: the French Revolution, 1936, etc. It was the triumph of *la bonne France*–France the generous, the model, the enlightened. And François Mitterrand, with his thin smile and discerning gaze, had the gentleness and experience of a benevolent father. I was keenly aware of this subtle mixture of eternal France and modernity, of small valleys and anti-racism, of Elysian dignity and *Touche pas à mon pote*. *France éternelle* had landed right in the middle of the country of TGV trains, US bags, and sentimental songs by Jean-Jacques Goldman.

This was, we were told, the Mitterrand generation. It was one more fortress keeping me inexorably shielded from the ghosts.

4

———◆———

ONE DAY, MY MOTHER found a piece of paper in her sister's files. That piece of paper, which bore the heading of the Ministry of Prisoners of War, was addressed to my grandmother. It was dated May 1945.

My grandmother probably hadn't read it until she herself had returned from Germany with her two daughters.

The family had been arrested a few months earlier in June 1944. In the convoy that left from Toulouse in July 1944—and in which Jews and resisters were mixed together—the women and children had been sent to Ravensbrück and then to Bergen-Belsen. My mother's father had never returned from Germany; it was presumed that he had died there.

My mother and her sister had learned that—though neither they nor their mother knew it then, and they were just little girls, anyway—their father (the father with blue eyes of whom only three or four photos remained, the father whose even-featured face resembled the American actor Paul Newman's, the father they pictured next to his own brother in the mountains of Galicia, where he'd been born, the two brothers who were like two versions of the same face, one harmonious, the other a mess), their terribly handsome father had spent his last weeks just a few steps away from them in the barracks, at the door to the barracks, on the walkways through the camp that had been built in the heart of the Bergen-Belsen forest in Northern Germany.

It was war, they had come back; he'd died one hundred feet or so from them without their knowing. They had grown up without a father, far from Northern Germany, returned to life.

It was war, there were the disappeared and the others, and now it was necessary to live, here, in France.

My aunt Pesia, my mother's sister, was the spitting image of her father! She was, as he must have been, magnificent. Even back then, in the camp, her beauty had saved her. With her curls, she looked just like Shirley Temple. For the little Shirley Temple of Bergen-Belsen, my grandmother received vegetable peelings and a little soup, too. She was so adorable with her curls full of lice. For the little Shirley Temple of Bergen-Belsen with hair full of lice, the world was, nevertheless, the camp, the barracks, the roll-calls, the shots, the dogs, the dead bodies, the thin tree trunks covered in snow. It was lingering at the doors to the kitchens, an imitation Shirley Temple, begging for the vegetable peelings and soup that kept a person going for a few days, a few more weeks.

And Pesia's beauty had survived the war. She'd turned into a terrific young girl, a motor scooter and all the rest, a well-formed figure, knee-length skirts, beehive hair, gingham dresses, Brigitte Bardot, Catherine Deneuve. It was miraculous, that face and body, smooth with no scars, no tattoo, nothing. That beautiful, tall young girl, so uncomplicated, who could have been an actress on the black and white streets of Paris Nouvelle Vague. Nothing stirred in her peaceful face, a Madonna, until her eyes eventually fell upon a law student in glasses, a student who became a lawyer, a lawyer who gave her three children with blue eyes like Paul Newman, and with those three children and the lawyer she moved into a big house-yard-Formica kitchen in the Paris suburbs, and to those three children, lawyer, house, and yard she devoted herself as was proper and good and normal to do.

But something was wrong.

Inside the house she tidied, she took care of the children. She took care of the far end of the yard, the tall pine tree that grew in the middle of the clipped grass; she trimmed the dark green hedges that camouflaged the outline of metal fencing. She no longer had Shirley Temple's ringlets; *au naturel* she would have, but she straightened her hair mercilessly every morning, strand by strand, and even the smallest curl could not escape.

She cooked, she invited people over, and sometimes we would go. She organized grand luncheons, interminable afternoons. In the dining room with glass doors that looked out onto the pine tree, the grandmother would sit at the end of the table, watching her youngest daughter without speaking. The grandmother, served first, who conscientiously emptied her plate, cleaned it, emptied it, nothing left on the plate, white, gleaming, the plate extraordinarily empty whenever she had been there. We, the grandchildren, were in turtlenecks and corduroy pants. That was the style in those days. Pesia's children had blue eyes like Paul Newman, and my sister and I had brown eyes like just about anybody.

Pesia served, cleared, straight hair and her remarkable face on which I recognized the same strange smile my mother had. She hurried around this way, dish towel, dishes, sauerkraut, kisses for the children, conversations, but when I looked at her I felt as if there were two Pesias. One for dish towel-dishes-sauerkraut-kisses-children-conversations and the other who peered with distress at the active Pesia while she, the other one, remained standing, motionless, silent, as if behind a glass bell, capable only of perhaps walking her hands over the transparent wall and banging on it.

In spite of the movement, the shouts, the noises of covers on the plates, and the lawyer's loud voice, the house was inhabited by this invisible duplication, and the atmosphere, the carrying out of actions, seemed to be in subtle slow motion, dilated. My cousins' blue eyes were not as bright as they could have been, their movements less defined. I found the shadow of the pine tree through the glass door gloomy. I liked my younger blue-eyed cousin; she was the one who

27

resembled Paul Newman the most, the one who hid under the stairs, at the top of the stairs, at the bottom of the stairs, in the wine cellar, the one who stayed stubbornly silent when we spoke to her, and who, when she did end up talking, had a strange voice, rasping, the voice of another world.

"At school they say I'm weird."

"You're not weird, Judith. You don't like talking, that's all."

"Actually, it's the not talking that they think is weird."

"And what do you say to them?"

"I don't say anything to them. I never say anything to them."

"Give me your hand, Judith."

"For what?"

"So I can keep it nice and warm for you. So I can give you powers."

"I watch them but I don't care. They can think I'm weird. They can laugh, jump, run . . . I watch them but I swear I really don't care . . . Hold my hand a little longer."

And I held her hand in mine, in the warmth, in the darkness, under the stairs. We looked at each other, the two blue-eyed/brown-eyed cousins. And eventually Pesia became afraid; she called throughout the whole house and came to force us out from under the stairs, but Judith said nothing, didn't speak. We were put in two chairs, our feet not touching the ground, under the grandmother's supervision.

"I don't understand anything she's telling me with her Yiddish."

I spoke softly to Judith; the grandmother didn't hear anything, she was deaf.

"Do *you* understand any of it?"

"No, Father and Mother speak Yiddish when they don't want me to understand."

"I know for sure I won't speak Yiddish in front of *my* kids, I'm not going to speak a language they don't understand."

"You don't know that, you can't know. You don't know if kids understand or if they don't. Sometimes they even understand a language that they *don't* understand."

My mother and Pesia returned from the kitchen. They each sat down next to their mother, facing us. They stayed like that, a strange trinity, the mother, the silent daughter, and my mother, who in spite of everything was smiling.

"Pechiou," the mother said, "go and get me the tea in the kitchen. Perla"—my mother!—"take out the papers, I'm going to make you the list."

The two women obeyed their mother's orders; tea, shopping list. She had only to wave her two wrinkled hands. On her left ring finger, she wore two wedding bands of white gold. The rings were too tight, making her veiny skin swell up. Perla and Pesia moved like Siamese twins, and this ancillary twinship was a continuation of their childhood and adolescence, when the two had slept in the same narrow bed, head to toe, feet and hands tangled, a single body.

I observed the reconstruction of this archaic alliance between the mother and her two daughters; it was an ancient scene—a zone forbidden to us—in which were reborn, intact, in their freshness and their violence, the invisible impulses of the soul and memory. There wasn't even a need for words, just the grasped hands, the laughter, the eagerness, the glances exchanged in secret, the mute disapproval; they had an entire well-oiled choreography in which we had no place. Besides, when it came to children—to us—the grandmother really couldn't care less. She had saved two other children at a different time with her own hard work, like two puppies brought to the surface with their skin between her teeth. The litters that came later did not interest her; she was—who would've guessed from looking at her, that wrinkled old lady?—a goddess of fertility who reigned without tenderness.

Sitting on the chair just across from her, I watched for the moment when my mother would become my mother again. When she would escape the zone and return to me as herself, full of warmth. And, finally, she shook herself free, crossed the boundaries of the magic circle, took two steps, and placed her hands on my cheeks.

Pesia remained on the other side of the border, next to the goddess, absent. Judith was quiet, absorbed by this spectacle. The lawyer continued to pontificate.

We left for Paris.

On the banks of the Seine, in the neighborhoods at the edge of the city, was a bric-a-brac of wastelands, old workers' hostels with their outdated cafés, buhrstone houses, and housing projects with façades that were already gray.

Everything had sprung up, been destroyed, and reconstructed without order. From time to time, between a house
and a low-income building, even a stretch of wild riverbank
would appear; unruly trees and below them the wide coursing of the Seine.

The faces of girls with shining lips on the flyers for erotic
telephone services posted crookedly on the walls, the calm
fishermen straight out of a Renoir film, the bar-restaurants
with striped awnings, white letters painted in a semi-circle
on their windows, blacks wearing boubous walking under
the sun, a man smoking a cigarette alone in the window of a
stone building, enormous among the small homes, the empty
workshops and broken tiles of a factory in ruins. There was
never the possibility of settling one's gaze on something, of
getting used to it. This was the *banlieue*, a landscape that was
incongruous, unfinished, stratified; holes left by buildings,
holes left by time from which returned, breath by breath,
the imagined memory of before the war, the fervor of rue
Lénine, the idleness of Arab cafés on rue des Fusillés.

At each new crossing, my mother would show me
the disappeared houses that had been destroyed or already
replaced. She was the attentive recorder of these transforma-
tions, ones that moved her as deeply as if she herself were the
landscape being changed.

And the Seine, massive and slow, would accompany us
on our voyage. It moved forward, bordered by warehouses,
then sandy riverbanks; its substance, its movement, and its
uniform color amid disparate urban plains were—before it

tamed itself at pont d'Ivry and entered Paris in majesty—a reminder of the elementary structure of lands and water.

It was a few years later that Pesia first attempted suicide at the Pantin cemetery. She had chosen a funeral at random, let the procession move farther away, and then she had arranged the bottles around her, swallowed all of the medications, and lain down with her arms crossed on top of the tombstone. It was there that the funeral parlor employees found her a few hours later, stretched out, lifeless. They saved her, of course, and nothing was left of her gesture except the ridiculous nature of her setup: a suicide in a cemetery. She was cared for in the same hospital where, a few months before, the grandmother had deteriorated in a room invaded by the shouts of children rising from a nearby school playground.

We waited for news about Pesia in the same hallway where we'd learned about the grandmother's death. The lawyer, for once, was silent. My cousin with blue eyes held my hand.

We remembered the grandmother's death throes: the way she no longer spoke or ate or drank for several days and then, out of the blue, how she'd sat straight up in the bed, settled herself comfortably into it, refusing the drip, and then had started screaming without stopping. Nothing could stop her anymore!

She screamed while together the two sisters rushed around the bed to try and take her hand, she screamed whenever the nurses would come in, holding their ears, and rough up her old body from which there was nothing left to draw, neither healing nor silence.

She screamed when I entered the room, dead with fear, almost pushed from behind by my mother who was standing in the doorway, and while I stood for a long time far away from the bed, concentrating on the games the children were playing in the schoolyard. She screamed at night, she screamed during the day; the other patients complained, it felt like being in a madhouse. The staff was completely disorganized, and the doctors didn't understand how this could be happening when she was lying helpless in her bed, her legs barely covered by the yellow hospital gown.

Perla, my mother, and Pesia, my aunt, would conspire together in the hallway, in the room, their heads leaning against one another; they'd each come to one side of the bed to caress the face resting on the pillow, but the grandmother kept her eyes and mouth wide open, straight up to the ceiling. She continued her monotone cry, wordless. She kept on like that for two whole days.

We watched mechanically as the nurses' aides passed in front of us, we heard the squeaking of their plastic sandals on the linoleum.

It was then we realized that the silence had returned.

When my mother and aunt came out of the room holding hands, their faces were white, their eyes dead. The hallways, fluorescent lights, and the hospital linoleum had disappeared, replaced by a barren plain enveloped in wind. They walked out of habit, but when they put one foot in front of the other it was as if they were weightless, in thin air; they had lost their certainty of place, their sense of time. They were each like a child who has just been born, incapable of fixing his gaze. The world was no longer standing up, it was once again a succession of incoherent injunctions, shapes, and sounds in the midst of which they were navigating by sight, indifferent. They had lost their translator forever. It was strange because the others fell for it: the doctors, the funeral home employees, the rabbi. They saw the beautiful faces twisted with sorrow, but that was normal, a testament to reverent filial compassion, and they accepted the faces as representatives of the people they were speaking to; they spoke with contrition and empathy, diagnoses, the size of the coffin. Deception! They had become tiny again, they no longer knew anything.

They were still holding hands the day of the funeral, their two silhouettes in the middle of a path where dust was swirling, covering with a thin white layer the shoes of everyone in the small group gathered around the coffin.

The sky was imposing: gray clouds raced across it and eventually blended into one another before each one left again on its own course. The trees, too, were moving under the gusts of wind. There was no doubt about it; this was truly weather for a funeral and the end of the world. I heard the rabbi talking about Warsaw, but he may as well have been talking about Mars, or Neptune, far-off planets, he may as well have been talking about Pompeii, cities swallowed up. I daydreamed about bodies frozen in lava; I closed my eyes, letting myself be soothed by the rabbi's lumbering voice.

When I opened them again, he was holding his hat firmly in his hands to fight against the gusts of wind, and he was already at "the tragic tumults of history."

Pesia and Perla weren't listening to a thing. They were staring, left of the path, at the little hole in the ground below the highway in which they'd have to let go of their all-powerful and stern goddess. It started to rain, and the rabbi had to cut his speech short. Everyone hurried into single file between the rows of graves to get to the hole where two groundskeepers were patiently waiting, leaning on their shovels. The rain whipped everyone's faces, people jostled each other on the path, umbrellas banged against one another in the air. The sand transformed into mud in which no one was able to move; a few tried holding their arms out like tightrope walkers on the back edges of the gravestones to try and escape the swamp, but they stumbled on the muddy ground. Even the bucket filled with dirt for everyone to throw on the coffin, once it had been lowered down, was drenched. The sand had turned back into clay and, in spite of the small pail they used, as people took their turn they stained their hands or faces with large black smears which they tried, despite the solemnity of the moment, to clean discreetly.

At the head of this procession, Pesia and Perla had thrown their handfuls of dirt almost distractedly, one after the other, without pausing beside the grave. They looked ready to flee, but they still had to form a condolence line at the other end of the path. The funeral director, wearing a sopping black suit, led them by the arm like a Chief of Protocol and placed them under two trees that were dripping. The line re-formed, we shook hands energetically, murmuring, hurrying to be done with it. My mother and my aunt, both soaking wet, shook hands, smiling like two robots, and in an instant the cortège went by and people started running, car doors slammed, and we repatriated Pesia and Perla into a car, the wipers flying over the windshield.

And it was over.

Later, as we climbed a deserted boulevard Voltaire, Pesia, huddled in the backseat against the cousin with blue eyes, began softly repeating:

"We abandoned her in her hole. She saved us and we abandoned her in her hole. She's all alone, freezing. We left her."

"We didn't abandon her, Maman. She's dead, she's buried."

"We abandoned her in her hole."

My mother said nothing. She looked out the window. I knew that in the unchangeable façades of the buildings, in their persistence, she was looking for the vanished comfort of her mother's arms.

After Pesia's suicide attempt, the people at the hospital had watched us return with worry. The screamers!

But she remained quite calm, shut up in her room. She would watch us enter, following each movement without releasing her gaze. She played along with the attention, the covers under her chin, water in the glass, the radio on the table during the night. She smiled, she said thank you. She probably wanted more than the covers or the radio: what she

really wanted was for us to save her. She left, fragile-look-
ing between the lawyer and the cousin with blue eyes, and
returned to the house with the pine tree.

During one of her convalescences, while she was sort-
ing through her papers and some of my grandmother's that
she had salvaged, my mother stumbled upon the letter from
the Ministry of Prisoners of War.

April 1945
Ministry of Prisoners of War
Department of Missing Persons

Monsieur,

*[With names that were so bizarre—the grandmother's was
Mendla, one could never make heads or tails of it, was it a
woman or a man?—they had opted for the most generic term,
Monsieur.]*

*The Ministry of Prisoners of War, Deportees, and Ref-
ugees is pleased to inform you of the liberation from BER-
GEN-BELSEN of Monsieur STERN OVADIA currently
awaiting repatriation.*

*Certain liberated individuals were able to leave ahead
of our correspondence and will have returned to their homes
when the present notice arrives. Please accept, Monsieur, the
assurance of our sincere regards.*

On behalf of the Minister
Director of Missing Persons

Paul Newman!

He'd been liberated, he'd been alive.

"Alive," my mother murmured to herself when she'd finished reading the letter, and that single word transfigured Aunt Pesia's living room; even the pine tree outside the window was less sad. "Alive," my aunt repeated, and once again—though by now our feet touched the ground—Judith and I were sitting in chairs across from them, watching the show.

The lawyer interrupted them, imperious. "He may have been liberated and then died right after the letter was sent. He may have died right away, from typhus, from who knows what. The British soldiers who liberated the camp were afraid of those living cadavers when they first saw them. They stuffed them with food, and the living cadavers couldn't handle it. They ate and ate but they couldn't handle it, so they died. That's exactly what could've happened. They liberate him, they put his name on the list of survivors, they write the letter and bam, he dies, but now there's no letter to fix the mistake. He's dead, typhus, something else, he's dead. At any rate, he never came back."

He spoke to them as if they hadn't actually seen the piles of dead bodies, had never seen the lost bodies on the beds, delirious with typhus, as if they'd never offered their heads to their mother so she could remove from them, for hours on end, the swarming lice, the lice of typhus.

Regardless, they paid no attention to him. Pesia remained in her armchair, elsewhere, and my mother had already gotten up to dig through the papers. She found three photos of Ovadia and spread them out on the coffee table. A portrait of Ovadia, Ovadia at the office with his colleagues in a suit and tie, the elegance of a Brummell design, and a candid shot of Ovadia arm in arm with people we didn't know on a street in Prague.

"He could just as easily not have died. Maybe he didn't want to come back, who knows why. He may have come back and not said anything. To start another life, without us."

And my mother grasped the photos in her hand, studying them, as if it really had been possible to find an answer in his frozen eyes, as if it had been possible for photos to suddenly come to life, leave their black and white trap, and come resurrect themselves in the middle of the living room. She looked at them like a child waiting for a miracle.

"He may even still be alive. Old, but alive."

"We should do what they do for missing children. Using the computer, they can make the faces look older. They recreate the child's face at ten years old, at fifteen years old . . . We could make his face older and give it to the people looking for Nazis, Wiesenthal and those people. They find Nazis, so they should be able to find Jews, right?"

We all looked at Judith, who had never talked so much. My mother turned the photos around between her fingers.

The man who until now had been a dead shadow had been alive; the letter told us that, and maybe he still was. This certainty transfigured the house in the suburbs. The living room was invaded by a presence that occupied its empty spaces. Behind our chairs, next to our bodies and our faces, close to Pesia's pained face, my mother's worried hands, near our feet, Judith's and mine, stuck to the floor, Ovadia had leapt from his place of exile. He'd traveled across spaces and years, he'd crossed borders, half-phantom, half-man, he had disrupted the normal successions of time and memory to appear before us (and this apparition was a whirlwind, new blood) on the brink of repatriation.

5

———◆———

WHEN YOU LOOK AT a street, at buildings, at façades; twenty-six years, thirty years—is that a little or a lot? When you move around a city, when, as if inside an untouched forest, you trace in it trails only you can decipher, when you go over and over the same pathways, when I walk and walk again in Paris, the stones, what are they saying to me? Walker, that's a distinctive piece of clothing you're putting on, the way it dilutes the lines of your body, the way it forgets your gender and what you're made of. That passing through me, who has become invisible, absent, are the particles of time, that they are giving me life, that they are exoticizing me, that they are imprinting themselves in me, surviving because of me, my body and pristine head, miracle child, carrier, just like there are water carriers, bread carriers, I am a carrier of stories, of names and telephone numbers. The senseless utopia that everything revives and inscribes in me for the simple reason that, armed with my post-war vaccine, I am me, *immortal,* and I will always remember everything.

The streets of Paris are fine streets, ones that do not tumble into ruin, ones that traverse the centuries indifferent to the wars, the disappearances, the collapses. The buildings of Paris are fine fortress walls, more or less whitened, and without too much risk the sentries of time can easily examine the stones to make ghosts appear in the middle of the city in motion.

So you walk. This walk was an apprenticeship. The streets, to begin with, had been full of signs, colors, and movements: this was rue du Louvre near the Seine in 1978. The red diamond outside the *tabac,* the fluted wicker chairs placed neatly on the sidewalk, the huge metal façade of Établissements Cain et Rheims—Silk Fabrics, the half-erased face of a pink and chubby baby drawn on a blue background against a section of brick wall: these were the solid, tangible signs which, in their sequence along the street, seemed like the materialization of a necessary order, the one belonging to the real life of adults. An order you needed only to look at, look at a second time, and look at again to rightfully be part of.

Then, gradually, the signs grew rich with knowledge, with disappearances, and in the same way that the depth of field can suddenly appear with greater and greater clarity in a cinematic image, on the streets of Paris and on the façades of buildings, the crowd of invisible details had congregated around well-known landmarks.

There were only a few of us to keep an account of these details that were inaccessible to the naked eye: hunters, tamers of phantoms, the sentries! Like sorcerers on a quest for underground water, propelled by their never-ending walks. They intermingle with the city they wander through until they become components of it as natural as the buildings, the domes, and the carriage entrances. They appear in the middle of a street, or at summer's peak in the sun-bleached courtyard of a certain old hotel, where the old stables still remain and have been transformed into storage rooms, and the wrought-iron lanterns swing from the ceiling of the stone vestibule.

I remember Sentinel No. 1, posted on rue Jouffroy d'Abbans. More rarely, rue des Morillons or rue Blanche. Sometimes place Saint-Sulpice. The sentry was a tall man, almost six feet, once brown-haired, now going gray. Distinguishing mark: a stutter. Familiar with the shadows of the Occupation, the uncertain silhouettes of the sixties. I met Sentry No. 1 when I was fourteen, on boulevard Malesherbes. He had feverish eyes, and he walked without looking around him.

Whenever we ran into each other over the years, always by accident, he would smuggle me secrets under the café table about a seedy cabaret hidden in the recesses of a staircase in Montmartre, the mysteries of empty streets in the 15th arrondissement around the Lost and Found Center, the long waits of his childhood near place Pigalle.

Sentinel No. 1 methodically paced around the city, hoping to make the vanished shadows reappear with the power of his panicked eyes. The shadows already existed in his silences and hesitations when, sitting across from me, he'd try to speak. "It was a bizarre place . . . it was a strange place," he smiled. He would have liked to say more; he couldn't, so he smiled to show his good will, but he never went further than "it was bizarre." And in order to say "it was bizarre," he'd take a deep breath, he'd speed up his delivery, so much that I believed it was only a prologue, but then he'd stop short, smile, and repeat more and more softly, "it was bizarre," as an excuse, an explanation. And as he sank back into silence, I saw a transparent cohort appear at his sides: traffickers and second-class actresses, runaway teenagers, dead-ends where abandoned children hung around. He'd shielded them, even in his silences, from the forced march of time, and the shadows accompanied him, intangible until, periodically (and I imagine this was also a way of getting rid of them, of sharing with other people the weight of their presence), he gave them a body of words and letters in the books he wrote.

On pages resembling photosensitive paper, the silhouettes extracted from silences and walks would appear, little by little, as if in a chemical exposure. They carried with them the sweltering days of the month of August, the province towns one escapes by car, and uncertain destinies, all of which—tenuous and paltry framework of history, sensation, minute, movement—would never have been able to be brought to life without his stubbornness.

I'd seen Sentinel No. 2, Jaro, hanging around the metal gate outside a building, looking at the garden and the lawn, and in front of the white buildings striped with shutters—from a moment of early nineteenth-century folly—in the middle of the rue des Martyrs. In those structures that were only several stories high, giving one the illusion of being in the provinces, Jaro had lived as a child during the Occupation. He'd fled in July 1942 with his parents on the day of the big roundup, the same day my father and his own mother, who were living at the end of a street a few hundred yards up, had taken refuge there. He had told me the story of his flight, and I'd told him the story of my father's. He'd taken a paper from the inside pocket of his overcoat, and on the back of a leaflet he'd drawn for me that day's journey, from rue des Martyrs to rue des Écoles. The crossing of the Seine had been an immediate relief, which he represented with a drawing of a smiling cat on a stone bridge. Decades earlier, the old man across from me had been a child-cat who wove in and out of the back alleys of Île Saint-Louis, eventually ending up in hiding with Father-Cat, Mother-Cat, and Sister-Cat in a maid's room perched high above rue des Écoles. And from those years, when the greatest danger came from a creaking floorboard, he had kept the habit of walking on the tips of his toes. He'd mimic this gentle gait along the closed train lines on boulevard Pereire, but he limped a little and from the back, with his disheveled white hair, he resembled an old elf.

He had enlisted a few students from Beaux-Arts to paint the walls with big brown-eyed yellow cats who would continue watching over him from the rooftops. He took me by the arm and pointed at them with a sweeping gesture:

"my lucky star." One day in 1943 when the parquet floor had creaked a little loudly, a few hours later there was banging on the door of the maid's room. Father-Cat, Mother-Cat, Sister-Cat, and Little-Cat recoiled, terrified. In the end, Father-Cat had opened the emergency window and Jaro had fled over the roofs, leaving the others behind him, huddled together.

He'd say to me, "I know what the quiet façades are hiding." Crouching on the roof that day, from high above Jaro-Cat had seen the minuscule silhouettes of his parents and sister put into a car; he had also seen, pressed against the gutter, the car pull away in the wide perspective of rue des Écoles and then disappear to the left on rue Saint-Jacques.

And on that sidewalk, where the presence of the black car and the small silhouettes had already been buried, people walked by, stores were being opened. This was the Paris he saw from an overhang, the streets carved in neat lines; the walls like stone cliffs absorbed the disappearances, enduring without a second thought.

High up, around rue des Écoles, he knew the incline of every roof, the cornices, the orange chimney blocks, the zinc and the slate, flowing with rain, spots whitened by the sun. Later, during the Liberation, he hadn't let himself be taken in by the city's return to normalcy. For him, it had never stopped being the place of flight, of rescue, and of swallowing up. Since then, he had been resisting—solo, an orphan—against the disappearances. To get his revenge he needed to see everything, to understand everything, to know everything about the simultaneous movements on the streets he observed—even when he was walking at the level of the sidewalk—in plunging panoramic view as if he were still perched on his roof. The invisible threads of motorcades, trajectories, the continuous stream of urban movement, limitless cellular river; people passing, buses, girls, horns, boys, *métros*, hair in the wind, old men, rustling, idleness, children, desperate people, bare legs, trees, conversations, monuments, burning sidewalks, clinking of machines, frantic hands, the dead and the living. He strove to control or even reroute this flow, a traffic controller of accidents and coincidences.

He told me the story of the blonde girl he'd followed one day in the mid-fifties as she was coming out of the Vélodrome d'Hiver. She had taken the *métro* to the Bir-Hakeim station and disappeared before he could approach her. At the time, Jaro, who had never gone to school and had never worked, was a professional chess champion. To find this girl again, he decided—the way one introduces a wonderful strategy but also one without any clear rational basis—to station himself every day between six and seven p.m. at the bus stop by 91 place de la Bastille. Naturally, after a few weeks, the girl stepped off of the bus. He approached her, told her the whole story, she agreed to walk with him, and off the two of them went around place de la Bastille, then to the left on rue Saint-Antoine. No money for the restaurant, they walked and kept walking, and they walked so much that they were stopped by the vice squad working undercover in the neighborhood, which at the time was a hot spot for soliciting prostitutes. Explanations were given, they laughed, they set out again. An egg at the counter to calm the nerves and it went on like this for part of the night, walking. They were very respectable. Then, before leaving, the girl swore to Jaro that she had never been to Vél d'Hiv', and had never taken the *métro* to Bir-Hakeim, but overall she enjoyed the story.

He brought me in front of buildings with two entrances, rue de la Bienfaisance, rue de Rome, rue de Cronstadt, and told me stories about dramatic getaways. He mimed the fugitive's dizziness, showing how, by getting in over there, and coming out over here, he'd thwarted the city's staid protocols.

And I, who felt that this was a power—the power of life and survival, resisting against the apparent order of the city, making things disappear and reappear at will without seeming to, pretending, as Jaro did, to be just an anonymous passerby in a gray overcoat while all the while, in reality, he was casting the nets of his knowledge over the mute façades—I learned, I watched, my heart and memory wide open, I wrote down the addresses, I retraced the paths.

And I defied—peaceful young girl, lungs filled, body exultant—I defied the course of time.

In the small streets behind avenue des Ternes, I walked alongside Sentinel No. 3.

He moved slowly; the slightest effort wore him out. He was going deaf, and only heard me if I shouted in his ear. We remained silent most of the time, or I'd listen to him speak without even trying to respond. We'd pass in front of Le Franc-Tireur café, the red brick Saint-Ferdinand's church. We'd climb up toward a quiet little village square, a stone's throw away from the turbulence of place de l'Étoile. On the *terrasse* of an almost provincial cafe, Sentinel Gérard—once a timid student at a boarding school in Normandy (fifties), once the respected leader of a small revolutionary group (sixties), once a clandestine emissary for that same group in the farthest countries (seventies)—Gérard, emaciated by sickness, would warm himself, eyes closed, in the sun. He'd stop speaking, appearing to be asleep, and then in a soft voice he would start again, and when his eyes opened after a few minutes, they held a twinkle of irony and tenderness that made me blush.

On the fourth floor of a building on rue Saint-Ferdinand, he showed me the windows behind which the former director of a group of foreign resisters, Adam, still hid himself away. He hadn't come to live there until recently, not knowing that on the street perpendicular to his there had once been a brothel, later transformed into a swinger's club, that was managed by a young woman who had denounced some members of his organization during the war. Gérard told me that one of his friends in the sixties, Pierre, *vibrant* Pierre as he called him, had decided one night to go straight to place des Ternes and bump her off, the manager, the ginger, in her brothel named after an opera singer. In the end Pierre had gotten himself drunk out of his mind in a bar, he had given up on killing the manager, and he'd come back to the Latin Quarter looking slightly pitiful. Pierre had since died, Pierre whose hero was one of the young people under the orders of Adam, the old man of rue Saint-Ferdinand. Pierre who had been outlived by the ginger manager, Pierre whose tall silhouette and dark eyes Gérard saw once more. Pierre's useless violence, the way he wanted to make others settle debts that could never be paid. "Born too late to fulfill his dreams of great fighting, and condemned to farcical repetitions, he suffered," said Gérard, who claimed to suffer from the same disease: nostalgia for History.

"Oh beautiful, grand, tragic history," he intoned in the sun on place Saint-Ferdinand, "beautiful history, beautiful scarf, I wrap myself, you wrap yourself, blood-adornment that you watch from far away . . . no splatters, no, just harmless shivers, indifferent to the breeze and tepid climates, you yearn for storms, a bovarism of catastrophes. Calm amplitude of the retrospective, you evaluate the choices, you hoard the dilemmas for yourself; horrified, so nobly horrified (so much you can no longer sleep at night!), you measure murders and battles; you enroll yourself, panting, in the race of marionettes, heroic, soldierly, martyred marionettes whose first names, habits, and addresses you know: cop, novelist, historian, empathetic spectator from the future.

"You live every life, you jump from one marionette to the other (the choices are endless). You're almost there, you're almost there, and you obviously never really get there. From the peak of your time, from the imposed end of your

linear time, it will remain unknown to you, sealed forever:
the insane minute swollen by the biting wind, the moment of
dislocation that is no longer inhabited by words or by memories . . . only the awareness of the body as a string hanging
over nothing, the painful, terrifying awareness of the frozen
body. And your heart hammers, thrusting fear along your
legs, open sphincters, your back is heavy with sweat, hunger,
cold, thirst, blood, cries. When all the world gives way, when,
in this desert, there is nothing left but this body and its fore-
seeable death. Tell me, what can we feel about that minute?
It's as if it was behind a transparent pane of glass and we are
knocking, we're knocking, eyes wide open, bulging, in vain.

"My little girl"—and he would stroke my cheek, in the
shelter of the sidewalk on place Saint-Ferdinand—"we all, all
of us, hold onto our beautiful histories, our tragic histories,
the ones that suit us, the ones that occupy the daydreams of
peaceful times, and we gently pull the strings, we coincide,
we get agitated, we occupy ourselves—*noble occupation.*"
And he laughed.

I knew, though, that despite his speeches, despite most
of all his weakness and his deafness, Gérard still dragged
himself to the four corners of Paris to visit those he called
his "old revolutionaries." They came from every country:
Romania, Poland, Spain, Czechoslovakia. For Gérard, that
geography of ancient fights was superimposed on the city's
topography, even covering it up: he would go to Hungary,
rue Amelot, to Poland, porte de Bagnolet, to Spain, rue Sor-
bier. He climbed into minuscule apartments, taking care of

papers, retirements, pension requests that even the fiercest of the old revolutionaries had to submit in order to survive. Then he'd turn the volume on his hearing aids all the way up, and in the half-light, in armchairs with old covers that were often the sole survivors of exiles and emigrations, he would scratch down a few details, a few dates.

He enjoyed listening to the broken, homespun French of his old friends. He knew quite well that the accents that had become so familiar to him, that could single-handedly evoke a multitude of distant landscapes, would soon die out like the transitional dialects of a tribe that has disappeared, and that one day he'd wake up with not one person left on the surface of the earth who would speak this way, and the idea of this loss left him more unhappy than even the prospect of his friends' "real" deaths.

For that wobbly language—as much as the faces, the photos, the autobiographical accounts taken down on copy paper—bore witness: it spoke of lost countries, of exiles, and each misplaced tonic accent, each error, was like a scrap snatched from life, a scrap of flesh, a scrap of straw, the accumulation of which had eventually formed those fragile nests just outside of Paris.

Janina, the Polish woman, was Gérard's favorite. She lived on place de la Porte de Bagnolet in a brick low-income building. She was Pierre's mother. After spending the war in France, she had returned to Poland. She had not returned to Paris until after her son's death. She spent her days between her bed and the single chair near the yellow plastic table on which she had her meals. The small room was always dark, the curtains drawn, a lamp turned on in the corner. In the dimness, Gérard could still make out her radiant violet eyes, the only trace of what she had been. Gérard would sit on the chair, his knee almost touching Janina's as she sat hunched on the edge of the bed. She could stay sitting like that for hours, her face in her hands, in silence. Gérard would wait.

Janina started speaking for herself. She compiled an inventory of certain episodes in her life, organizing them in a different order depending on the day, without regard for the chronology. The damp walls of the prison in Warsaw where she'd been locked away between the two wars for illegal activities and communist propaganda, the alignment of the twenty-five birch trees along the path in front of her father's house, the sparkling of their green silver leaves, the sweat that ran down her legs one August day in Lyon as she carried weapons hidden in Pierre's baby carriage, weapons intended for an attack on German soldiers. The lost look of the young boy to whom she had given one of the grenades, the stealthy way he hid it in his pocket, the feeling of conspiracy like an unending road that unfurled in front of you, the congested train platform at Gare de l'Est when she'd fled from Poland in secret and disembarked in Paris for the first time, the return to the Polish People's Republic, without her child, without Pierre, the fervor of the marches, the slogans, the building of socialism, Pierre raised by his father coming for the first time to see her in Warsaw, their loneliness, the ruins of Warsaw, understanding and letting it truly sink into your head that there was nothing, of all the side streets, avenues, gardens, of that entire city, nothing that remained except sand and stones. Warsaw 1945, a swamp of ruins, and at dusk, jumping from the burned-out façades, rowdy groups of orphaned children who threw stones and thought they saw fork-footed devils snaking in and out between the pieces of wall. They would surround the devils and she-devils, saying, "Jew, Jew, devil, Jewess, she-devil, where are your forked feet?" They would spit, cross themselves, and disappear again behind the collapsed walls. It was a landscape of apocalypse bordered by the coursing of the Vistula.

Janina stretched out on the bed and turned her head toward Gérard. "You're not so deaf when you make an effort." And Gérard, the little man from Normandy whom the promise of revolution had once dragged like a hurricane out of the cloistered universe of the woodlands, Gérard, who was ever after bound by the implacable boundaries that illness had drawn inside him, Gérard found in those hours with Janina, in that pitiful shoebox apartment, beside that old woman who had seen everything, the certainty that a movement between souls was possible, one outside the limits of bodies, places, and time.

He told me everything, leaving nothing out, in the bright sunlight on the *terrasse* of the café at place Saint-Ferdinand because, though he didn't say so, he hoped that later, when Janina had died and he too had disappeared, whenever I passed la Porte de Bagnolet, among the cars, next to the signs for the *périphérique*, looking up at the top floor of the pale brick low-income building, I would be able to bring to life inside me the sparkling of the leaves of the twenty-five birch trees that ran the length of Janina's father's house.

6

---◆---

So, it was the end of the twentieth century and my mother had started searching for her father.

That old president was still here, his face petrified like a mummy's. As death grew near, he didn't conceal as much, and he no longer tried claiming nothing was wrong, though perhaps that was just for show. He even seemed to be giggling at what an evil trick he'd played: Generation Mitterrand, what a joke! In the era of computers and the first portable phones, that old president was more Fourth Republic than ever. I had only to see him—prim and impenetrable against a background of Elysian gilding, reserving his enthusiasm for prejudiced writers' most rancid pages, their sentences about the great France of old, scheduled and straight-lined, standing at attention—and I understood, little by little, just how naive I had been. This "former" naiveté exasperated me, but it was also a moving example of extreme youth's messy hopes, those same hopes that make you jump and run without fear of being split apart, as if your body and spirit were overtaken by an uninterrupted movement impossible to contain. I had been very naive: the post-war had never really happened.

Like a stream that continues flowing invisibly under a city's paving stones—even though outside things were heating up, things were changing, there were protests, the settling of scores—the old friendships, division, and promises persisted and shaped what was happening, without anyone on the surface (the surface of daily life where the years complacently went by) noticing the actual flow of history. And it was strange to see the old president seem to forget in the last months of his reign his most recent metamorphoses (into the good father from your hometown and the humanist for a new France) and rediscover—though an old man, though he was fragile but combative and sharp, and even mean—the conservative and scheming young man he had never ceased to be.

The president had gone stale. The expiration dates were coming closer, it must be said, and time was whipping by at greater and greater speeds, just like emails and text messages. At first we were surprised; we were suspicious and then overjoyed by the feeling that we were carrying out a marvelous ritual which eventually, over time, would be rid of its magic and become an unremarkable daily act.

But from now on the speed, the ubiquity, and the disembodiment went without saying; this was how we would learn to live.

7

——◆——

It was the end of the twentieth century and love had emerged from out of the mouth of a boy I was introduced to one night, Daniel. "That's hurting you," Daniel had said to me. There were ten of us at dinner and I was all over the place, talking spiritedly about one thing and then another; I'd forgotten as I was speaking, too loudly, too intensely, the grief that came with it. Vodka, I drank it, cigarettes, I smoked them, and, I thought, with panache. And he was right there, uppercut, "That's hurting you."

He was an analgesic sorcerer, this Daniel! Immediately, something had unwound on the inside of my body. All he had done was say those few words while looking at me thoughtfully, and the tumors of fear and worry—invisible, transparent tumors I was not immediately aware of until the very moment they were set to disappear—had dissolved all at once. The pain, the sadness, the hardness of things, and my own hardness were obsolete relics that had been ripped out of me.

First there was the abandon of his brown body, asleep at a diagonal on the bed. And as months went by, then years, there was the time each evening when I would glue myself to the black railing outside the window and watch for his return. In front of me, the roofs soared upward as far as the eye could see, as did the sky. We were all waiting together, the roofs, the sky, and me, for the thin silhouette's arrival on the corner of the narrow, sloping street that led to our place. As soon as he appeared, I'd start whistling like a caged bird calling for its liberator. I whistled silly melodies to make him laugh, sad melodies to make him cry. He'd stop on the sidewalk below the railing and answer by whistling back. These exchanges would last for a while until he'd rush up the staircases to climb the floors.

At night, burrowed into a narrow red sofa and facing one another, we'd murmur to each other for hours like two children conspiring unbeknownst to the adults. We closed ranks against fear; we vowed mutual, unconditional protection. Then, tired of words, lying down, this time next to each other with our heads touching, we'd look up through the glass roof above us at the shades of the darkening sky.

Days, days, months, months, years, years. In real life it was passing by, but under the glass roof, in our shared childhood, time was long and marvelously repetitive.

Daniel, his fragile body, his unchanging gentleness, was my first line of defense against the world. I could leap, jump, growl, and creep slowly toward him, somewhat menacing, my claws in the air, but he would always escape like an elf; like an elf he'd get scared and suddenly, out of his mouth and eyes, his laughter would unfurl.

The library was my other high wall. Between the white wooden shelves, the cruel century lay stacked, compiled, and collected. A paradoxical wall I had patiently constructed, an incongruous assemblage of book-bricks: memoirs, stories, and biographies by the hundreds; silent people whose groaning, assertions, commitments, and betrayals nevertheless invisibly invaded the room. Destruction, Gulag, Ghetto, Komintern, Revolution. Nothing escaped my inquisitions.

I learned topographies, itineraries, networks, and trajectories by heart. I reconstructed lives, looked at photos, and cross-checked the evidence. I juggled accumulations of names and histories until the encyclopedic polyphony of tragedy eventually took shape in the peaceful Parisian apartment. As for the horrors themselves, I read every one. Bombings, camps, Sonderkommandos, ruined ghettos, failed revolts, deaths by the hundreds, the thousands, the millions, bloodlines hastily buried, futile attempts to flee. Fascinated, I observed the apocalyptic hand of History shattering human hope even in its most wretched corners.

But even in the most horrific of those readings, mixed with the terror, in the abandon and the morbidity, I felt vaguely that there was also an element of pleasure. The horror I visited every day by proxy accentuated the sense of vitality in my own existence and an awareness of its miraculous permanence. And perhaps all of those dead people, in order to make it that much more joyful, were hiding in the whistling that welcomed Daniel's arrival each evening.

And how bright the apartment was where we lived on that small street in Montmartre, how radiant and perfectly proportioned. How ideal a setting it was—with its soft light, skillfully chosen paintings, its impeccable mixture of simplicity and good taste—for remembering. And in the end, how the grime of evil inevitably came knocking on the dependable filter of glass roofs and patterned objects.

I had come down the sloping hill to meet him. I caught sight of him on his way up: the quick gait, his brown edges cut out on the buildings behind him. I ran toward him, light, as light as a shadow. He stopped. He watched my body coming closer, already double. Where did his gaze find that grace? He had understood. He welcomed the joy, the joy and also my turmoil.

I heard the child who came stirring in her cradle, which was placed a few yards from the sofa. From the street I also heard a car starting, workmen renovating an apartment in the building across the way, and also, once in a while when the street was calm in the hot hours of the afternoon, the far off humming of the *périphérique*.

The child was moving in her sleep; sometimes she would wake up without me noticing and I would find her immobile, still clammy from sleep with her eyes open, for she, too, was attentive to the murmuring of the city. She looked at me and it was as if she were waiting for me to translate this murmuring for her, waiting for me to come up with an explanation for this acoustic chaos. So I would whistle again, imitating the starting car, the hammering of the tool, and she would laugh.

She learned to walk, to speak. I held her to me, breathing in the smell of her hair, which had grown naturally into the tonsure of a monk, and at nightfall we danced one against the other, banishing in our body-to-body the melancholy of the sky dying down outside the window. Then I'd lie down next to her, waiting for her to fall asleep. One night, sitting on the edge of her bed, I watched her pupils rolling beneath her eyelids; she was almost asleep. She suddenly reopened her eyes and reached her arms toward me.

"Maman, you will save me," she murmured, looking at me.

"My *bijou*, yes, I will save you." I closed the door and glanced at the library. Its radioactive matter was glowing in the darkness.

And I was radioactive, too.

With Daniel, we would go into Paris. We would walk in the middle of the night. Rue Saint-Vincent and rue des Saules were covered with an immaculate snow that muffled our steps. We went without a sound, without a shadow, like fraternal specters relieved of our biological bodies. We pushed our explorations as far as the boundaries of the 17th arrondissement. Under the gray of the sky, on those wide streets with their unobstructed views, an immense and disparate story was building in which, via links that appeared to be random but were, beneath the surface, necessary, the expensive and blended generations of Plaine Monceau appeared one after another: the Sunday austerities of Catholic families, the heroic silences of wise young resisters, the boredom of autumn Sundays in apartments crudely lit by a halogen lamp.

For us, this was the nostalgia of the 17th arrondissement! For us, there were memories of huge rooms that were dark even in the heart of summer; in one corner of the kitchen, the maid would have fleetingly fallen asleep, her head on top of her arms. The glass in the stairwell windows, and everywhere was the silence of families, the mother reading in an easy chair, the sons measuring, one foot in front of the other, the dimensions of the unending hallway. They were ours, the orangey reflections, the balanced frames, the doors with twenty-five little panes; they were ours, order and harmony and silence. We thought we had the power to understand the street signs perfectly, as well as the buildings: Prony, Fortuny, Meissonier. We had to return constantly to the same windows, to see how things were arranged inside Villiers, Meissonier, and Prony, and most of all to understand the *movements* behind the windows, the succession of generations. The structure of families unfolding into life in the quietness: parents, children, staff. The lunches every day around the table, the father reading the newspaper, the mother scolding the maid, the children scratching their heads. The children, April 1920, April 1950, April 1986, their return to Lycée Carnot for afternoon classes, looking at the tree leaves on avenue de Villiers as they walked.

To Daniel—my shadow, my soul, my brother—I would say how important it was to understand what switches on, what turns off; what comes in, what goes out; what leaves, what stays. Daniel and I had to make the rounds on rue Fortuny and avenue de Villiers and painstakingly tie the threads together because I knew, and I told him this as if it were a secret, that the stone we were looking at—such an unusual texture, the holes spread along its surface like so many dilated pores on a face—concealed the mysterious movement of life.

As for my mother, she was looking for her father. She was like a little Gretel who would search pebble by pebble for a way out of the woods, carried by the stubborn belief that she would find her home again. Except that now the pebbles weren't in forests, they were on the last floor of the archives at Fort de Vincennes, in the basements of the archives of the Ministry of Armed Forces. She crossed Paris, climbing up and down staircases, a valiant soldier. She outwitted the temperaments of archivists worn out by her beginner's zeal. She put up with their contempt, the boxes laughingly thrown onto the table, the irascible sarcasm ("Of course, Madame, if you're not in the *habit* of looking through archives . . .").

She took good notes. She filled notebooks. Prefecture of Police: STERN OVADIA, born 26 October, 1901, Warsaw, Poland. STERN OVADIA, son of Emanuel and Amalia STERN, profession: employed. STERN OVADIA, first known residence in France: 20 rue Riquet, Choisy-le-Roi. 1.76 m, 70 kg. Oval face. Blue eyes. Languages spoken: French, Polish, Czech, German, English. STERN Ovadia, born in 1901 in Warsaw, of Polish nationality, was married on 6/13/30 in Paris 5th with his fellow countrywoman JANKEIL Mendla, born in 1905 in Rozan. From their union is produced one child: STERN Perla, born' on 5/9/1936 in Paris 12th, French by declaration, registered at the Justice Ministry under No. 8677 X 36. Request for naturalization received 16 October, 1936. Request denied for both: lack of assimilation into French culture.

She left the archives of the Prefecture and descended the sloping rue des Carmes. She arrived at the Maubert-Mutualité *métro* and caught up with the Seine via rue de Bièvre. Behind Notre-Dame, she took refuge in an empty garden. Sitting on the bench, eyes closed, she relieved her gaze from the columns and lists; then, house by house, she looked across at the old homes of quai d'Orléans on the other side of the Seine.

She had the letters he'd written in Yiddish, Polish, and German translated into French, and like a good and diligent student, after each translation she placed the letter and its French version in clear plastic sleeves that started to accumulate on her desk.

Translated from German
Prague, September 30, 1928

Dear Ricky,

As you instructed, I went down to the offices of American Express, Dlouha 10. They told me they might have a need for me and that they would give me an answer soon. I've decided to keep renting the room in Dejvice after all. It's not that expensive, and in case American Express works out, at least I will have the room to start off with. Thank you for your help and your letter of recommendation.

All my friendship.
Your devoted Ovadia.

Translated from Yiddish
Prague, October 5, 1928

Darling Mindla,

American Express is giving me work for at least a few months. The stipend is adequate, enough to save for Paris. On Sunday, we went with Roth to take a walk in the park that people here call Petřin. It's Paris before there was Paris! There is a sort of miniature Eiffel Tower that overlooks the park, which overlooks the city and, in particular, the Petit Côté neighborhood, Malá Strana. The room I've rented is outside the center of the city but on a very quiet, wide, and pleasant street. I under-stand Czech completely, but I still make mistakes when I'm speaking and I often mix it up with Polish. Darling Mindla, I hope that your dear family is doing well. Your dear father, your dear mother. Prague is only for now. I look forward to finally being in Paris so I can prepare for your arrival.

Your Ovadia.

Translated from Yiddish
Prague, November 2, 1928

Darling Mindla,

Don't be unfair, sweetheart, I accepted the contract for a year because it seemed to me a better way to prepare for our move to Paris. No, staying in Prague without you is not what I want! It's true, I feel comfortable here. In the old city, certain build-ings have a double entrance, a passage leading from one to the other. Sometimes I walk all the way to the Charles Bridge without following a single street. I pass from building to build-ing. It's a whole science, the art of cities. But Mindla, I want to be with you. In Paris! And if you don't believe me, I will write it to you thousands of times, I will write it to you without stop-ping, so much that your dear father will become dizzy from seeing the postman delivering all of the letters to you.

My love.
Your Ovadia.

Translated from German
Prague, December 10, 1928

Dear Ricky,

As you saw with your own eyes, the room is comfortable. No, I am truly not complaining about my living conditions. In fact, I find it miraculous that in a few months, in part thanks to you, I've been able to find work and a place to live in a city I didn't know. Mindla is getting impatient. She would like to leave Poland, her family, and for us to finally be together in Paris, the way she has always wanted. I don't really know what she's hoping for with this "new life," and sometimes, dear Ricky, I'm not sure I'm capable of giving her exactly what she may be expecting.

Your devoted Ovadia.

Translated from Yiddish
Paris, July 18, 1929

Darling Mindla,

I will pick you up directly from the station, then. Don't hesitate to send me a telegram once you are on your way to let me know you've left. The room is bright. It is not in Paris but just next to it, a small town called Choisy-le-Roi. It is quite pretty. The Seine is not far. I will be working on avenue de l'Opéra, that's where the American Express offices are. Don't hesitate to send the telegram. Either way, I'll be at the station on the platform. You'll recognize me, won't you? Darling Mindla! Your loving Ovadia.

Translated from Yiddish
Paris, July 28, 1936

Dear brother,

Thank you for your letters. The little girl is doing well. She is out of danger. Perla, yes, like our mother, may her memory be blessed and sanctified . . . Dear brother, there is so much worry in your letters. Of course you should leave the country, send the little boy to me. I'll do everything I can to take care of him. We have moved to Paris. The apartment is small, but we'll always be able to make it work. I need to find out which papers need to be completed. I will send them to you, don't worry.

Your loving brother. Ovadia.

Translated from Polish
Paris, January 3, 1937

Olek my friend,

I went back to the Prefecture of Police to get a visa for my nephew Adam, Icek's son. They are requesting a guarantor in Poland and, naturally, Icek's guarantee is not enough. Would you be able to act as guarantor for Adam? He's the only one I can bring over and Icek is getting more and more worried. He would like to get Adam out of the country. I hope to get your answer very soon, dear Olek.

Your Ovadia.

Translated from German
Paris, December 5, 1937

Dear Ricky,

Everything is going well for us here. You ask me if we ever go out. Cinema, theater? Very little for us. No money, no time, Ricky! Paris, city of lights; that's for the others, not for us. I am very preoccupied these days. From our country everyone is asking me for visas, passports. People are panicking, they want to leave. I do what I can, I send the money orders, I run around to the different offices, I get stamped what needs to get stamped but everything is still out of reach and I can't manage to do anything for anyone. Not even for my nephew Adam, Icek's son who you met in Lvov. I feel the fear rising, and I can't stand being here with my family so well-protected while others in Poland and Germany would jump over the borders in bare feet if they could. I hear horrible stories about the current atmosphere in Poland. Hateful posters on the street, the numerus clausus, attacks in public. It's a strange time, Ricky. The thirties in this century don't look very good to me. I hope that Prague resists!

Your devoted Ovadia.

Translated from Czech
Paris, July 3, 1941

I am writing to you in mid-flight, Ricky! And in Czech as an extra precaution. We are leaving Paris for Toulouse. We will be there with the children at Mindla's sister's house. Our temporary address: 17 rue de Rome. I hope you will be able to leave Paris very soon. Don't hesitate to join us.

Your devoted Ovadia

P.S.: I'm leaving the ticket with the concierge. Her face worries me. I really think it's urgent that you get out of Paris.

The letters were sitting on my mother's desk: there were the white pages with the French translations she had recopied in her steady handwriting, and on the grandfather's brown sheets was the disorder of different languages, the passage from Hebrew letters to the accumulations of consonants in Polish and suddenly the polished heights of German capitals. The missives became less legible as the years went by; he wrote more quickly, rushing, as if the frenetic wind of danger were pushing against his neck. The letters pulsated, and as she went about her most trivial tasks I'd see my mother glance discreetly at the white and brown pile, the incandescent pile.

I monitored her slightest gestures and her slightest looks because she had abandoned me: I interested her less. Still, I became a very nice young lady. Polite, presentable, independent. Had I not been at the same level as the miracle of her survival? But my mother no longer looked at me; she had gone back to her childhood, and having no other choice, I ran behind.

Soon she became bolder, she began writing to Germany, to Poland . . . She wrote letters in clumsy English. She asked for information, birth certificates, death certificates. She closed herself in her office for hours on end to worry over those interminable correspondences. They answered her in German, in Polish. They didn't know. The archives had been lost, the archives had been burned. But she found the addresses of other archives.

On the plastic table in the kitchen, she would spread out the letters she'd received, her notebooks filled with columns and dates, and she would start the same letter again, writing the address on the envelope in round letters to be sure the letter would not get lost in transit.

Then one day came the call to action. She had decided to travel, to see "for herself!" First step, the last camp: Bergen-Belsen. She wrote to very friendly archivists—it was inevitably the Germans who were the friendliest, in proportion to their sense of guilt, and this feeling would continue to grow as years went by—who warmly invited her to visit in person to examine the documents regarding the camp's liberation.

Everything started at Roissy, direction Hanover. In actual fact, for me everything had started at the Golden Circus Bar in Terminal 2D with three glasses of lukewarm vodka, the only remedy for my horrendous fear of planes. The takeoff in particular, the precise moment when the airplane left the ground, plunged me into unrestrainable terror; there were a few seconds of vertigo during the diagonal rise toward the sky. The abrupt acceleration, the plane's taking flight, and its tumultuous passage through the layers of clouds were among, I was sure of it—and my lips were dry, my hands clammy, my heart on alert!—the most uncertain of wagers.

I latched onto the flight attendants' faces. I interpreted their smiles, their expressions. It was exhausting work, watching endlessly for the moment of the fall. And naturally, every time, the landing was a renewed miracle.

The airport in Hanover was empty. So was the town, in fact. Just the blinking of bright signs. Faintly, through the taxi's open window, I heard Madonna songs playing from loudspeakers set on the corner of pedestrian walkways.

The buildings were new, the streets were clean, the cars were prudently aligned behind each other. On the highway, I looked at the green fields. We could also see houses with red roofs, neatly positioned cows, and, sometimes, a silhouette in knee-high boots, immobile among the trenches drawn by tractors. It was as green, red, and plastic as a Playmobil toy landscape. I could almost have taken the houses in my hand, moved them around as I liked from one side to the other, and placed the little man astraddle on one of the roofs. In the taxi, we listened to the metallic voice of the GPS giving the driver directions to the hotel in the middle of the countryside where my mother had reserved two rooms. The landscape before our eyes was transformed on the computer screen into long, thin, pixelated rectangles, and I watched us with fascination as we navigated along those virtual fields and roads.

After straying onto the streets of the small town of Celle—receiving from the GPS, the farther we strayed, directions that were closer and closer together and more and more authoritarian, *zur linken, zur rechte*—we finally arrived in the middle of a paved courtyard bordered by stately buildings made of gray stone.

Two uniformed grooms rushed toward the car and, each opening one door at the same time, they offered us an arm to climb out. With the same swiftness, they packed our luggage onto a gold trolley and then followed us until we reached a hall crammed full of imitation Louis XVI paintings and furniture. An enormous crystal chandelier hung from the ceiling; its transparent pendants chimed faintly as they touched. Behind the reception desk, two blonde women with impeccable makeup smiled at us rigidly. I looked at my mother and motioned for us to flee but it was too late: we had landed in all of the splendor of a German luxury hotel.

We were escorted to our rooms through corridors lit by electric candles. The rooms resembled what, to the German imagination, probably evoked seventeenth-century France. Canopy beds, flowery drapes, assorted footstools, and bookshelves filled with trompe-l'oeil books.

It was clearly indicated that smoking was prohibited, our escort explained to us in perfect English. Perhaps he was trying to offset the threatening nature of the small placards placed at regular intervals around the walls of the room, on each of which a cigarette was crossed out with a huge black X and the word *verboten*. Obviously, as soon as he left, trembling with fear, I ran to lock myself in the bathroom, opened a skylight above the jacuzzi tub, and hurried to light a cigarette, all the while carefully examining the ceiling to try and spot the inevitable smoke detectors. I hadn't even smoked half of it before someone knocked on the door to my room. I began frantically stirring the air in the hopes of making the smell disappear and then innocently opened the door. The hotel manager was on the threshold, imperturbable. With a gracious smile he said, "Shall I remind you, Madam, that we have a strict policy regarding smoking and no smoking."

"Yes, yes, absolutely, this is something I can quite understand, I heard you perfectly," I sputtered.

He smiled. "Thank you Madam."

As I closed the door, I decided to get my revenge by attacking the mini bar and began looking for it without success. Finally, after a long half hour, I suddenly pressed on a painted panel depicting a pastoral scene in which, against a Roman Campagna background, two young shepherds dressed as lords were embracing each other among their sheep. And just like in the most brilliant spy novels, under the pressure of my hand the panel abruptly turned around on itself, uncovering a stockpile of small, perfectly organized bottles of alcohol.

Later at dinner, in the room where we were, of course, the only guests, I regretted my misjudgment. I was afraid I would fall down in front of the hotel manager, the same as ever, who now stood behind our chairs ready to pounce, to refill our plates, or to anxiously wonder whether the meal was going well.

"Is everything fine, Madam?" To be honest, everything was not fine for Madam, who was smoking cigarettes on the sly and who had guzzled down two mignonettes of vodka in fifteen minutes. No, really, everything was not fine: this faux chic could have been the decor in a low-budget erotic film, I was terribly nauseous, and my mother, sitting across from me, her head lowered over her plate, was obediently eating the endless sequence of dishes. She was afraid of the hotel manager.

Foggy from the alcohol, I felt that in spite of everything we had to try to fight against this stucco kitsch, this gastronomic overload, against the hotel manager's servile posturing; we needed to take a machete to this monstrous scene in which my mother and I were losing our grip.

It wasn't very subtle, but the first thing that came to mind was the following sentence, whispered between the salad and the potatoes and the garlic leg of lamb: "Mother, what time is our appointment at the concentration camp tomorrow?" I cleanly separated out the syllables in Con-Cen-Tra-Tion Camp as if I were hoping for a sudden explosion that would annihilate the manager and send him crawling on his knees to clear the table as fast as he could, that would return the walls to their natural plaster state, disintegrating the porcelain plates and the imitation painted masterpieces. But none of these things happened, and my mother settled for answering me between two conscientiously chewed bites of glistening potatoes: "Nine o'clock. The archivist is expecting us at nine o'clock."

"Some more wine, Madam?" Without hiding my belligerent intentions, I interrupted the minion who had already raised the bottle to refill my glass by waving my hand. "No, thank you very much, sir."

"And how are we getting to the Con-Cen-Tra-Tion Camp, Maman?"

"A taxi, I think," and my mother jabbed two pieces of roasted garlic with the end of her fork.

"And could I suggest, Madam, to have a look at our dessert menu and shall I allow myself to recommend some of those desserts." In my opinion, he was doing it on purpose. I simply shook my head without taking my eyes off of my mother. "No sir, thank you very much."

But my warlike passions were no match for my body's weaknesses. Reeling, I stood up from the table and ran to take refuge in my freezing room (like the castles of ruined aristocrats where appearances are maintained but the heat is only turned on for two months out of the year to save a little money, or perhaps this absence of heat was simply respecting the rules decreed by a stern nineteenth-century naturopath who had concluded that souls and bodies needed to be tamed with a bit of rigor). The fact remains that, shivering, I relinquished myself to a repugnant intestinal chaos on the immaculate ceramic of the jacuzzi bathroom.

I was frightened being alone in that room. Bent in half, I dragged myself to the connecting door that opened into my mother's room. I glued my ear to the wood of the door: everything was quiet. I peeked under the door; there was no light. I pushed the handle; the door gently opened. I took a few steps; there was only the illuminated beam coming from the door behind me that weakly lit the room. I moved forward, and then I saw her. My mother, pale in a white nightgown, sleeping curled up in the middle of the bed. She had arranged the photos of her father in a semicircle around the pillow: Ovadia at the office, Ovadia in Prague, the close-up portrait of Ovadia. The grainy material of the photos shone strangely with the effect of the light; they encircled my mother's head like a glowing, protective halo. I came closer again until I could hear her breathing, I lay down at the foot of the bed, curled up in her same position, and waited until morning.

The next day, my mother asked the taxi to drop us off in the forest a few hundred yards from the entrance to the camp. The road led straight through the pine trees. The sky appeared from between their somber mass like a narrow gray net. My mother went in front. I was unable to walk quickly. When she got too far ahead, I'd run to where she was, then she'd leave me behind again and I would run to catch up. I took a strange pleasure in this race, it was almost a game: I exaggerated my slowing down and speeding up. I tried without success to break the walking rhythm my mother had instinctively adopted. I didn't want a straight and linear step, though that was the very one I knew she was searching for again, the vibration inside her body. I heard the even sound of her heels on the path, her feet crushing the residue of moss, twigs, and small stones that went flying. I would have liked her to suddenly turn her face toward me, but she was sucked in by the straight line running along the black trunks.

"Maman, wait for me!"

I was no longer sure if I'd actually yelled, maybe I had only whispered it. The words expanded inside me, the way the shadows of the trees were expanding, their branches outstretched over our path.

"Maman, wait for me!"

I had a cramp, my back was sweaty, and this time I had shouted, I was certain, because all of a sudden the sound of the forest, the wind, and the bird calls went quiet. In this silence, she abruptly stopped and reached out her arm toward me. It was what I'd hoped for from the beginning: she took my hand, and I stayed several steps behind her. I felt her warm fingers against mine, and she dragged me in her wake until the entrance to the camp suddenly appeared, a large naked plain surrounded by forest.

On the side was a concrete building in front of which a middle-aged woman was shuffling back and forth. As soon as she noticed us, she came over to greet us.

"Hello, my name is Inge. I was waiting for you. I'm thrilled to welcome you here."

The newspeak was starting again.

With authority, she led us into the concrete building. This was the exhibit center, the archive center, and the multimedia center, she explained to us in her enthusiastic English. She talked about all of the visitors to the camp, among whom were numerous scholars who had come from all over Europe because Bergen-Belsen was taking part in a European program called "*Se Souvenir Toujours*" or "Remember Forever." They spent, on average, an hour and a half in the museum even after a long visit to the camp itself.

She reeled off all of these things as she descended a flight of stairs that led us to a room in the basement. On the walls were displayed enlarged reproductions of photos taken by the English during the liberation. Suddenly her face grew solemn; she slowed her step and reassured my mother that it was a moment of great emotion to welcome a child of Bergen-Belsen here. A flicker of compassion passed within her eyes, she twisted her mouth a little bit, and after having very meaningfully squeezed my mother's arm, she continued on with her guided tour. There were computers, books, photos; we could search, scan, copy; there were lines of archives for miles and miles, the equivalent of an entire Amazon forest, she explained with a laugh. As she said this, she pushed forcefully on a swinging door and paraded us before the metal library shelves on which, in fact, thousands of black and gray boxes were crammed together. She pointed to one shelf: "The Camp's Beginnings," then another, "Deportations, 1943." She took another step, "Civilian Population in the Area Surrounding the Camp," then with another step, "Liberation Committees." She had the garrulous congeniality of a real estate agent.

My mother smiled politely, turning her head left and right, agreeing when it was necessary. "Here we are, here we are," Inge suddenly whispered. She stopped short in front of several boxes identical to those we had just passed. Delicately, she unwound the string around the first in the pile and took hold of a few sheets that had been placed on top of it ahead of time. The brown paper was growing tattered on the edges, and Inge held the sheets out to my mother, who passed them straight to me. I didn't know what to do with them, so I put all of them on a small plastic shelf and all three of us leaned our heads over as if it were not a pile of paperwork but a living and fragile baby. There were columns, names, dates of birth. It was the report by the French Mission for Repatriation and Research, which was in charge of keeping a record after liberation of the living and dead among the French deportees. One of the pages was entitled "List of French Individuals Whose Trace Has Been Lost Since April 19, 1945."

Between Arthur Cuvillier, born in Amiens on 07.17.13, and Jacques Dahaux, born in the Loiret in 1925, we saw his name. What was most likely, Inge explained, was that those *without a trace* had died after the liberation and then been buried in the communal graves without having been identified. Those *without a trace* were simply those without a grave, in other words.

My mother quickly raised her head. "Yes, but we don't know, their trace really may have been lost, we don't know what happened exactly to them. They might be dead. They might be not dead." Despite her halting English, she had said these words with such a stubborn fervor that the positive, rational Inge straightened up and looked at her in disbelief. Inge was speechless. She was beginning to understand . . .

But she immediately composed herself, smiled wide. "Well, well, let me show you other documents." The smell of mold leaking out of the cardboard boxes and the millions of tattered brown sheets were stirring my stomach. I was pulling out of Inge's crazy race. I mumbled, "I'll wait for you outside," and went back up to the visitor's center. I responded to the dozing librarian who greeted me in German with a movement of my head and sat down in front of a computer.

I tapped on the keys distractedly; I was bored.

I opened Google Earth and typed in Bergen-Belsen, and suddenly an aerial view of the camp unfolded on the screen. I saw the roofs of Celle, the ones in the two villages of Bergen and Belsen, the fields cut in geometric forms, the stretches of woods. I saw the roof of the memorial where I found myself, and even the perimeter of the camp, which was sprinkled with dark rectangles. I zoomed in over a few yards of ground. It was the imprint left by barracks that had been taken down and where the grass had never regrown. I zoomed out; there was more. On both sides of the empty field that the camp had become, there were other slanted rectangles, not as many, but wider: the communal graves. And all around, in a wide shot, was the unmoving summit of trees. I stayed for a long time in front of the screen to look at the panoramic view. So long that I was almost sleeping with my eyes open: the image was getting blurry but I no longer even made the effort to adjust my gaze to make it clear again. I let the spots move before my eyes and envelop me like a colored haze. My mother wasn't coming back. Walking like a robot, I passed by the librarian again and climbed back up the steps.

I returned to the free air and crossed the camp's borders.

It felt good to move forward under the sun, to let my eyes rest on what was nothing more than a large clearing, to move forward in the grass step by step, to follow the stony paths, scanning the explanatory signs letter by letter without putting the words back together, to put one foot in front of the other a little more, to feel the sky above me and to feel nothing except its blue liquid, the shakings of the wind. So I went forward. Finally, after a while, I lay down without knowing where I was.

My head hurt, my head was spinning. The clouds, the magnificent clouds, were moving majestically above me and I felt every inch of my body's contour: the long line of my legs, my roller coaster fingers, the weight of my head against the earth. I fell asleep. When I woke up, I lifted myself up halfway and saw my mother's shadow coming toward me from the other end of the clearing.

She took a few steps and stopped, turning her head slightly left and right. She set off again. I saw her completely, then she disappeared, hidden by a mound of grass, and I could only make out her torso or her head until, finally, she emerged fully once more. She strode on. She was walking in her own footsteps again. She didn't see me, though there was nothing unusual about that because I didn't exist. Not yet. She came close to the edge of the camp, the trees, she touched the trunks, she looked at her hands, and she turned and walked in my direction. I now saw her face clearly: closed, inaccessible.

A few yards away from me, without so much as glancing at me, she squatted down. Her coat was dragging on the ground in the grass and her legs were spread far apart. She was crouched like an animal, like a monkey, like a wolf, like a dog. She was as small as a child. She looked around her and I realized she was searching for her sister's presence, her mother's. She was looking for her pack. In that moment, she could have pulled out a rusty bowl, lapped from it without a spoon. She could have devoured invisible scraps of bread. She could have stood up, stepped over the cadavers, she could have pushed away the ones who came begging for her soup, she could have been a threatening and monstrous child. Why she was crouching, she didn't know. But seeing her in that empty clearing, I realized—and the force of that image was such that my head spun, I had to close my eyes and stretch out completely against the ground—that she *had* been a monkey, a wolf, a dog. That she *had* devoured, stepped over, pushed away. She had been a threatening and monstrous child. Here was the root, the red-hot iron against which none of us—not me, her miracle, the houses of Paris, the repetitions of rue Caulaincourt, or the rescue attempts— stood the slightest chance. Swept away. The possibility of return was a mirage.

Under the autumn sun, in the middle of the vast clearing, I felt penetrated by a sadness that was so brutal, so desperate, I couldn't move. There was no longer anything to do but stay there, stretched out, to measure the regular path of my blood, the beating of my heart, the accelerations of my pulse, and to feel myself contained by the limits of my skin. To no longer move an inch lest I encourage suffering, lest I pave a way for it into each fold, each ventricle, each cavity that it would progressively contaminate over the course of its journey inside my swarming and open body.

In the silence we heard shouting. It was Inge, running clumsily toward us because of her heels, which were getting stuck in the grass. She brushed aside the leaves with her arms. She reached us out of breath, disheveled. Long strands of hair had escaped her chignon and were hiding her face. She suddenly seemed younger, almost a young girl, her cheeks reddened by the sprint.

"I found this for you, I found this for you," she repeated. Then she stopped talking, stunned by our statue-like immobility; we looked at her in silence. She started again more timidly, "I found this for you," and her hands were still twitching but only a little, and the leaves were trembling in her fingers, probably because of the cold. My mother looked at her without seeing her, almost squinting; she was seeing beyond her.

"Documents from Buchenwald about your father, before he arrived here."

"Yes, yes," my mother answered mechanically, still crouching.

"Just have a look, look at this," and she was almost pleading with my mother to take her papers, to hold them in her own hands. To come back.

"Yes," my mother said again, and she stood up heavily.

The wind picked up all of a sudden, and around us the branches and leaves were writhing, tight together.

Again, all three of us found ourselves gathered around leaves that the wind was threatening to tear out of Inge's hands at any second.

The texts were in German. Some were typed, others handwritten in tall, round letters. He had even filled out a few forms himself. Inge translated out loud in English. He had arrived at the camp on August 4, 1944. He had been registered on August 6, 1944 under the ID number (*häftlingnr*) 69646, between David Wajeman, 69645, and Paul David, 69647. He had with him the following objects and sum of money: 2 *goldene Herrenuhren eine mit Kette*, 1 *gold. Ring mit Stein*, 42,000 francs. He had said he weighed 70 kg and that he had the following medical history: 1916, *Rippenfellenentzündung*, 1936, *Geisteskrank*, 1940, *Ischias*. He answered to the following description:

Grösse: 174; *Gestalt:* stark; *Gesicht:* lang; *Augen:* blau; *Nase: gerade; Mund: grind; Ohren: absteb; Zähne: vollst; Haare: braun.* He spoke Polish, French, German, Czech, and English. He had been assigned to Block 51. He had then left Buchenwald for the Hecht Kommando, between Salomon Roth (*häftl. nr* 69644) and Charcoun Eleazar (*häftl. nr* 69655).

The last sheet was not a sheet, it was a small card in French.

STERNE Owadies
Born 10/24/01 Poland
Residence in France: Toulouse
Bergen-Belsen Camp
Trace lost since April 19, 1945
Source of Information: Search Bureau

"Trace lost," my mother murmured thoughtfully. "*Time* lost," I added. It beat along my finger, my heart, the blood, the pulse . . . The lines on her face were even, dug into the soft and warm material of her skin . . . I felt the freezing weight of the wind on my back as strongly as if it had been bare. In the midst of her light brown eyes, dark and opaque spots had emerged, drawing a complicated image over the iris. She grazed my shoulder; she wanted to hold onto me but her hand fell gently down. I didn't move; Inge had taken back her papers, hesitant. At last, she took a deep breath. She wanted to leave; we were suffocating despite the fresh air. "I need to put this back in the files, stay as long as you like. I'll send you copies of these documents." She shook my mother's hand, returned her errant strands to the chignon, made a military about-face, and I saw her move away as awkwardly as she had appeared, her heels sinking halfway into the ground.

I wanted a flying carpet to get me out of there. No returning to the woods. No going back to the hotel. No taxi, and no airport, either. I wanted to fly away from the middle of the clearing, to flutter without feeling a thing, to turn over in the air, to see the tops of the trees from above, to no longer weigh anything. I didn't want my feet to touch the ground anymore and I wanted any trace of me to be lost, too.

In reality, though, there were still the forest and the hotel. The gastronomic menu, the muted head waiter. There was the taxi, the Hanover countryside, and the airplane.

The small child at the house, my child, needed to be washed; she needed to be fed, kissed. She needed to be held far away from the blaze. I brought her to Parc Monceau.

I watched her as she ran along the straight paths, between the statues, around the fountain and ancient columns. She couldn't yet manage to coordinate all of her limbs: she would go with her arms in front of her, head leaning back. She leapt and fell down onto her feet. She screamed in her immaculate outfit. She pulled off the buttons and fought as she rolled in the grass. It was barely four in the afternoon and yet night was already starting to fall. The orange light illuminated the façades around the park. Under the fire, they had the appearance of a theater backdrop. Colored bands of pink and red sprawled far across the sky. The silhouettes of parents and children gradually became dark, and as they went back and forth between the violently lit merry-go-round and the candy kiosk, they didn't appear to be real. The women were carrying their teenage daughters' sneakers and the men grew bored, watching them from a distance. As if in a dream, they walked in silence to the rhythm of the darkness that was settling in.

Sitting on my bench, I wondered whether I was really there, a silhouette, one mother among others, or if all of this—the spectacular sunset, the bouncing shadows racing one another—was only a reflection of a life that had been dreamt, one that was intangible. My child was coming toward me. I saw her two dark eyes advancing. I felt the heat of her face in my hands. I saw the speckled, greenish skins of the statues behind us. Behind the gates, Paris had faded into the night. Parents and children left the park in small bunches; the guards whistled for the closing; on boulevard Courcelles, the cars' red and yellow headlights formed a crackling thread.

Paris had faded into the night and we were alive; unbelievably, unjustly alive.

PART II

To the East

1

I am afraid to go and meet You
But more afraid not to
Now I am amazed by everything,
And now in everything I sense destiny.
Alexander Blok
(Translated by G. McQuillan)

LEAVING THE PRISON IN Warsaw, I realized I had lost my identity card. It was February, and at four p.m., it was already dark. We had filmed a few scenes of a former political prisoner's return to the halls of "his" prison. Pressed against the bars, he puffed on his cigarette and searched for an answer to my question about his "most significant memory" from his imprisonment. It was a pathetic question, a pathetic plan for someone returning after twenty years, but he had kindly thought it over for a few minutes because, after all, I had brought together a whole team for the filming, and considering that the cameraman, the sound engineer, the assistant, the translator, and the prison guard—whose palm we had greased to get authorization to film for a few minutes—were all waiting patiently for him to speak before they either started the camera, gave him an opening, or began translating, he really needed to answer.

I was tired after spending the whole day asking him about his life, and I was looking forward to finishing. So I asked, the translator translated, he answered, the translator translated, and bing, that's a wrap. With his red silk scarf knotted around his neck, and his emaciated head, he had the look of a Polish aristocrat past his prime. He smiled and said, "I read, I read constantly. Pasternak, Dickens, Tolstoy, even Balzac, I think." I didn't even need to wait for the translator to finish. I had understood and was instantly awake. In the midst of dead dates and timelines, here was the "Open Sesame." I forgot about the piece I was filming on the Polish democratic opposition under communism, I forgot about the work schedule, the days beginning at dawn in a sinister hotel and ending at nightfall as we shot eerie views of the city. Time as something locked down and mapped out was forgotten, too, for I was in the very flow of life: "the cry repeated by a thousand sentinels," "the call of hunters lost in the big woods." It was Balzac and Pasternak thrown like a bridge from him to me. And I thought of the books I'd pile up around me before I closed my eyes at night—I was a little girl with sure instincts—like an invincible building protecting my sleep. I also thought about the story of Varlam Chalamov, a faceless *zek* saved from certain death under the ice in Kolyma thanks to a position as a nurse's assistant, who found *Swann's Way* on a hospital bench. Proust in the Gulag, the miraculous journey of books building a parallel world next to real life, a world unconcerned with death and time and history, unconcerned with limits. The materiality of the pages, volumes transformed into images, thoughts, getaways, and rescues spinning a refuge-thread as protective as a mother's watchful eye that men clung onto from one generation to the next; an invisible thread by which they still could recognize each other.

And it was this tenuous thread that had suddenly appeared, altering the routine, the piles of questions and the weariness at the heart of this prison where those condemned by tsarism, then by the German Occupation, and finally, by the communist regime of the Polish People's Republic—and sometimes they were the same people—had been imprisoned. Okhrana, Gestapo, UB.

So Roman Baljewski smiled again, and rather than telling me in detail how in this very prison he and his fellow Solidarity members had refused the agreement handed to them by Jaruzelski's regime—their freedom and the freedom of other political prisoners in exchange for leaving political life and no longer harassing them with their petitions, their union, their amusing desire to be free—instead of mentioning his heroic gesture, which I knew about already, having read about it in books, used it to prepare my note cards, and ruminated on it as I thought of all the questions I intended to ask him, instead of all of that, he began, as if he were simply following the thread of the interview, reciting a poem in Polish. I did not understand the poem. But I heard the music, and it was like a primeval language, a language before speech, before words, where only modulation existed. He kept his eyes fixed on mine, his head moving gently to the rhythm of what I supposed was the end of each verse, and even the operator with the huge camera on his shoulder was nodding, hypnotized by what was a babbling, a prayer, a formless nursery rhyme of reassurance and hope.

Now and then I recognized syllables of the song rising up among my cells, whistled ones I'd once heard exhaled by my grandmothers, the Polish of lullabies, the one murmured in secret behind the walls of Haussmann buildings. I almost would have taken Roman Baljewski's hand; I would have clutched it, caressed it, stroking his fingers, but one of the guards jangled his keys. The half hour we'd bought was ending and we needed to get going, fast. Ultimately, the prison was no place for poems. We packed up our things like entertainers being asked to leave; Roman Baljewski had not moved. He watched us idly; there was no sound except the noise of our crates and the shouts of prisoners in the corridor next to us who were pressed against the doors of their cells, drawn by our presence.

We gathered again in the courtyard. Baljewski followed us in silence, surrounded by the guards. He was smoking in huge puffs, his mouth tight around the cigarette. He listened to the jokes told by the guards, the sons of his own guards. A little lost, he looked at the silhouettes of the trees encircling the walls whose branches cut through the dark blue of the sky. A large automatic door opened. Outside were the streets of Warsaw, the tramways shining in the night, and people running from one sidewalk to the other, bound together by the invisible wave of their movements. There were straight lines, right angles, spots of color, and we were standing, almost squinting, the way you do after coming up from underground, at the edge of the world. Bravely, Baljewski moved away and we saw him release himself, anonymous, back into the stream of living people. We wandered around, filming shots here and there of lit-up storefronts, old men with lowered heads, geometrical perspectives, the tramways flying by. In the sky we could no longer make out anything except the birds coming and going as they traced wide, murky curves.

Unbeknownst to me, on one of those sidewalks lay my identity card with my photo, my address, and my date and place of birth trampled underfoot by the Warsaw pedestrians. My photo, my address, and my date and place of birth, 30 April, 1971, Paris 10th arrondissement, had been abandoned thousands of miles from the Sacré-Cœur, thousands of miles from my mother's eyes. That card was the condensed and unexpected representation of a return made in silence, almost in spite of myself, traveling backward through the invisible tunnels of time. The brutal return to a land I had never known and had never left.

I came back to the hotel, rising up in all of its ugliness—at one time the avant-garde of socialist luxury—along the banks of the river. Behind the automatic door in the hallway lit by neon lights, the bellhop, the doorman, and two idle receptionists watched me enter with suspicion, afraid I would try to speak to them. I went straight into the restaurant area, which was watched over by a melancholic blonde who dragged her worn kickboxing shoes over the floor as she drifted between three tables occupied by an illegitimate couple, an old man in a suit curved over his bowl of soup, and three quiet Spanish tourists. The waitress took my order absentmindedly while she glanced at the couple who were pushing their adulterous explorations further and further: the bright-eyed woman was stroking her companion's bare forearm, and he was getting closer, inch by inch, helped by the alcohol, to the pair of weary breasts coming halfway out of her dress. The Spaniards didn't miss a moment of what was happening and they laughed softly, nudging each other. Only the old man lapped at his soup with a dignified air, and I noticed his right eye fixed on an imaginary line at the edge of the synthetic fabric tablecloth.

The food at the hotel suited me perfectly, more in its matter—the gelatinous texture of meat and potato fritters—than in its taste. Its blandness was a strange cousin of the dishes that invaded my parents' table three or four times a year on holidays, and whose one-dimensional white flavor—far removed from gastronomic subtleties—was, and rightfully so in France, like a discreet reminder of an incomplete assimilation. In fact, the vodka I was swallowing from pairs of tiny glasses glistening with ice crystals had the same propensity for "non-subtlety": an abrupt alcoholized current that invaded all at once, penetrating the body with drunkenness without any natural progression.

After several tiny glasses, I struggled to collect my arms, then my legs, and went back across the room. The Spaniards had run off. The couple couldn't hold on any longer: the woman was squirming with anticipated pleasure as she closed her eyes. I brushed against the mumbling old man's chair. I distinctly heard the word *kurwa*, "whore" in Polish, then I heard it repeated, without pausing for breath, *kurwakurwakurwakurwakurwakurwa* . . . The blonde was sitting down again in a corner next to the door, waiting for the time to pass.

I walked over to the elevator. The bellhop, the doorman, and the two receptionists watched me spitefully. I took refuge behind the elevator doors. I saw my face reflected in the mirror, looked at the two dark eyes looking back at me, and told myself that this was a bad look, a face as sad as this would get you in trouble during the war. I saw my face diffracted under the influence of the alcohol and my fear, *kurwakurwakurwakurwakurwakurwa*, a face that came from somewhere else, one that would have been examined and scornfully itemized. One eye here, one eye there, a mouth that was too large; this was a face all on its own, and the loving look that rested on it—the only thing providing it with unity and meaning—would have been ripped away.

That night on the way back to my room, I realized that the city where I found myself, Warsaw, was the same city whose map I had learned in Paris, book after book. So, that night, as I leaned out my window looking at the Vistula pinned under the ice, I also realized that the familiar streets of my nights as a child were glimmering a few hundred yards away.

They shone in the night, behind the many buildings; they wound around somewhere behind the commercial spaces where cylindrical metal towers rose up, unreachable, and behind the oversized avenues invaded by the crazed herds of cars.

The next day I walked toward them. I held the map of Warsaw folded in quarters and I unfolded it while I stood under the winter sun. The sun warmed my cheeks, but I didn't want to be warmed because I needed to cut through— without warmth, furiously, at the risk of no longer being able to move forward—the transparency of the air. On the map the streets were tangled; I mixed up Jeruzalémaká, Paríska, Dlouha, Bonifraterska. I stayed rooted where I was for a few long minutes to unknot the black routes, the parallel and perpendicular lines, the outlined curves. I couldn't grasp anything on this map. The space depicted with dark strokes and colored spots—orange for monuments, green for parks—was impossible to transpose onto reality. I couldn't imagine my body being there.

I passed a park, a deserted square where a man sitting on a bench was crying in the sun. I took a running start to cross avenue Jean Paul II and found myself at the foot of a building whose white and gray archways signaled the start of rue Anielewicz. A blue sign in the shape of an arrow pointed the way to the monument exactly three hundred yards away honoring the heroes of the ghetto. Under the archways' vaulted ceilings, women wearing headscarves knotted under their chins were keeping watch over stacks of clear jars filled with honey and some kind of red jelly. All of the stores in the recesses of the archway were closed. Shots had been fired at the metal curtains forming rounded arabesque shapes. The emblems were in an old handwriting, black on a white background. I clung to the details, knowing I had crossed an invisible boundary. I walked more and more slowly. I arrived in a large square surrounded by modern buildings a few floors high. In the middle of the square were a garden, a few trees, benches, and off to one side I noticed the dead faces of an imposing bronze sculpture. On the empty streets between the buildings, I saw the names passing by: Miła, Zamenhof, Gęsia, Nalewki.

I felt the weight of every step; I was a diver or an over-perceptive astronaut, but the planet I was discovering wasn't the one I was seeing. The few silhouettes that were hurrying down the sidewalk, clipped out by the sun, were mirages: the woman with a dog, the child in the white anorak amusing himself by limping, the three teenage girls coming forward to greet me by holding their interlaced hands out in front of them. I had to push my gaze through them, as if they were made from the misty matter of clouds, as if they could be cut through, disintegrated, as if I could go and look beyond the buildings, beyond the silhouettes, to *my* topographies that I knew by heart, my old maps where if you took rue Zamenhof you'd run into rue Majzelsa, the maps where rue Gęsia led to rue Franciszkańska. I did my best to cross through the bodies and the buildings' light plywood, to pierce the morning silence so that finally, *finally*, superimposed on the old streets, the dark movement of the crowd in its shapeless bustling would appear, so that, with beggars' implacable strength, the details of a face or a shoulder in flight would latch onto my retina. And so that I would be among them.

But nothing came. The girls continued on their way and I heard the rumble of cars coming from allée Solidarność. Nothing, there was nothing. Only the buildings, the people passing, and the noise. I was gradually becoming Alice in Wonderland; I was shrinking. My legs were truly becoming minuscule.

I leaned against a wall to draw out from inside me the traces left by the crowds of the dead. Those thousands and thousands of words I had stored up inside my head, nestled between my living cells, those words in which the faces, names, and bodies pushed over the bridge on rue Chłodna became packed together, sticking to one another. The texts that had been buried and found, all of those images in my sleep that I'd hoped would return to life—like cells in culture kept in a vegetative state until they're plunged into the appropriate growth medium—spreading out as they broke through the peel of time to be reborn at last, out from within me.

I came across barbed wire and low-income buildings, and sprung up in their midst was a synagogue. It had been, the writing said, a synagogue and a stable and a hayloft and a merchandise warehouse. It had been renovated. It was green, it was pink, repainted; the doors were closed. It was green and pink, a leftover from the counterfeiters. I walked around the synagogue and was ashamed to be there, a solemn surveyor of the wreckage. After some time, I realized that on top of a brick building on the other side of the street, the photos of dead Jews were watching me. They had wobbled and then hoisted the photos against the windows, sticking them above the sidewalks, above the tramways and electric wires. A man with a beard was staring at me, as were the father, the mother, and the two children, and also a young girl. Dozens of photos on the façades displayed for everyone to see. The photo of the man with the beard was small; it had been made to be held in one's hands or stuck inside the pages of an album, but it had become immense, a folklore relic, improperly scaled like those unending avenues where the wind marched by in gusts.

I entered the courtyard of one of the brick buildings and immediately recognized its dimensions: the narrowness of the courtyard, the red brick walls, the eight stories, the windows heaped on top of each other. A deep square vault. I raised my head and my chin pulled into alignment with my neck: far away, at the very top, was a fenced-in square of clear sky cut out between the bricks. The images slipped out of me like verses. They took possession of the courtyard, flowing smoothly to attach themselves to the four walls: specters of useless and abandoned objects, open suitcases, scraps of fabric, scattered papers. They slipped out of me or escaped from under the earth onto the sunken cement slabs and asphalt lids. They ran behind the silence and immobility of walls the light couldn't reach, thickening the air and bringing the menace closer. The gray mothers, the gray children with no one to help them, the gray mothers, the gray children, I'm repeating myself, the gray mothers, the gray children, and this became a song and I took shelter behind its repetitions because I was afraid of the real apparitions right in the middle of the courtyard under the fenced-in sky. They were trapped in blurry clusters at the mercy of evil, no one to help them.

My vision fleeing, I put my hands in front of my eyes; it was invisible.

Outside, around the building, I climbed over small grassy mounds. At the highest point were structures from the fifties that had been built as rationally and evenly as barracks on top of the rises in the earth. I climbed up and down between the complexes. In the hollows under the hillocks, the paths were lined with trees and children passed on bicycles. I stopped to look at them and sat down, my back pasted against the slope. They looked at me, too, laughing. My mind was drifting, and night was falling. I suddenly stood up. I understood the meaning behind the mounds placed like anomalies in the midst of this city that was flat, so flat. I started digging with my toe. The children were no longer laughing; they watched me curiously. I began using my hands and kept digging. I didn't need to go very far and quickly pulled up a piece of dirty stone. I removed the dirt, cleaning it with the sleeve of my anorak. It was red brick, the kind used in buildings before the war. The ruins—stones, debris, human remains—had not been smoothed away: they had stayed here, loose, just a few inches under the grass. The children started their arabesques on the path again.

I stuffed the stone into the pocket of my jeans and took off running back to the hotel. During my run, this time without me knowing, I had crossed the line of demarcation that brought me back, far away from the edge of the precipice. I bolted like a rabbit and the city continued to sink on top of the cemetery.

Later, my assistant and I went to visit another former dissident who was living alone in a little house around forty miles from Warsaw. The assistant was chewing cloves; their nauseating odor invaded the car. I had spread out a map on my knees to find our way. At the end of a road tracing straight through fields, we entered a forest. All of the trees were covered in snow; it had started to melt under the sun. Drops shining with light fell regularly from the branches and were crushed on the windshield. *Pic-poc, pic-poc*. It could easily have been the enchanted wood in a fairy tale; the gaps between the trunks uncovered white stretches out of which a green patch would emerge from time to time, a tip of vegetation that had made its way through, fighting against the weight of winter. The air was sharp and light, as if each drop of melted snow were the cheerful harbinger of the thaw. But when we arrived at the end of the road where Karol Bielinski was waiting for us, the river behind him was covered entirely by an opaque layer of ice.

He smiled strangely, with either shyness or irony, probably both, as he approached our car. I got out clumsily, which made him smile even more. Very soldier-like, he leaned toward me and kissed my hand. Then we followed him toward a wooden shanty whose porch had been covered with a plastic tarp. There was a table surrounded by benches and we sat down. Bielinski and I were across from each other, and the assistant a little off to the side. We stayed wrapped up in our coats. Bielinski was wearing a thick jacket that was too big for him; the sleeves covered up half of his hands. He spoke French perfectly.

"So, what is it you want from me, mademoiselle madame?" he said very quickly, and immediately his mouth—which I saw in detail because I didn't dare look him straight in the eyes—contracted into a teasing smirk. Almost instantly—and the transformation did not escape me, because I was staring as if through a microscope at the details of his faded lips —it turned into a facial expression that I had just enough time to tell myself was rather cruel.

I had just enough time because I had not yet been able to respond when another man appeared suddenly from inside the cabin. He resembled a huge animal torn from sleep. His knit cap was pushed halfway down his forehead and he was moving slowly. When he came to examine me up close, scrutinizing me like an inanimate object, I realized that he was disabled or insane. He was perhaps thirty-five years old. The black strands of hair escaping the hat framed a round, asymmetrical face that immediately produced a violent desire to get away from it, to turn one's head.

In a very gentle voice, Bielinski began speaking to him in Polish. Without saying a word, the animal removed his eyes from me and sat down on the bench next to him. He sighed noisily, placed his head between his two hands, and started staring at me once more.

"This is Heniek, my son. We woke him up. He's going to stay with us."

The appearance of Heniek had at least given me a brief respite. Yes, what was it I wanted from Bielinksi? Why had I come all the way into the forest looking for him, interrupted his hermit routine, and woken up his son? What unsatisfied hunger nestled in my ribs (I imagined an insatiable and unmoving dark cavity amid the other moving organs) was needing to be fed, needing to be filled, that I should want nothing else except to have him tell me stories? That I should want to learn, as I did that afternoon—and I immediately felt the path this information took from my ear into the folds of my body where it eventually landed—that during the war in 1943, when he had been placed in an orphanage near Moscow with other children whose parents were at the Front, he had worn a military coat with gold buttons on the epaulettes that his mother had gotten for him.

"Her husband, my father, had been arrested, disappeared in the camps. Before the war she was a nurse, like Lara in *Dr. Zhivago*. She met the man whose name I carry, a Polish communist, Bielinski. I was a good little Soviet and arrived in Poland in 1947." Bielinski was speaking like a telegram, though I knew from having been told that he had been able to leave crowds hanging on his every word when he spoke, an intractable rhetorician who used the same fierce intelligence to denounce the regime that he had earlier exercised as a Marxist-Leninist zealot.

"My adoptive father, in other words, my father, was the minister in the early fifties. I would see him at night in the big apartment; his face was gray, preoccupied. There were trials and suspects. One night, a kid's story now, I was maybe nine, I tell him that somebody, a neighbor's father, is very suspect, a reactionary enemy. His gray face turns white and he slaps me hard enough to knock over a bull. It was the only time; he'd never laid a hand on me and he never did again. And he was the *minister* of this government, the very person who locked away the reactionary enemies. My mother looked at me, pale, and took me in her arms. She had seen

108

reactionary enemies arrested! She was a real Soviet woman, tough to crack. Later, when my father was already dead, I was serving my first prison term and she would come to see me. She had big, blue, innocent eyes, and she'd leave with little notes I wanted to get to the outside. She hid them on the inside of her houppelande sleeves and passed proudly in front of the guards. She had big blue eyes so they let her go. They were intimidated. Lara, I tell you."

"La-ra-i-tell-you," Heniek repeated phonetically. He had a very unpleasant high-pitched voice, "la-ra-i-tell-you, la-ra-i-tell-you." Still watching me, without even turning toward him, Bielinski had taken his son's hand in his own and was gently tapping a rhythm on the table in time with the meter of the words: "laraitellyoularaitellyou." With each syllable he thumped his son's hand and his own on the wood the way he would have with a two-year-old child. He smiled and then started speaking again, while Heniek continued his chant, and the two voices wove together like the two hands. "Yes, prison, several times, years. One had to be heroic! What I mean is, one was supposed to be heroic, like Daddy and Mommy. The genes . . . If you think about it, for them there had been Spain, the war, all of that. It was our turn to be the heroes! But heroes weren't so tragic. Prison was just prison, there was no death at the end of it. There was a guard, always the same one, who used to greet me warmly whenever he saw me coming back. 'You again, Pan Bielinski. Back home again? Come in, come in, we were waiting for you.' When he left for retirement, he came to see me in my cell. He was almost sad; he knew that I'd come back and that he would no longer be there to see me. He was right. I came back a few years later, two years, and he wasn't there anymore."

"Hewasntthereanymore," Heniek burbled, "hewasntthereanymore." It was the bastardized echo of Bielinski's voice, a senseless repetition that matched the house deep in the forest and the banks of the frozen river where Karol Bielinski's life had come to collapse.

"Heniek is hungry," Bielinski suddenly announced. He stood up and arranged blue plates on the table along with six serving dishes he had filled with herring, meatballs, small meat *crêpes farcies*, pickles, beets, and eggs. Heniek began eating like a sprinter, his head lowered, eyes almost closed. He had already pushed away his plate, grunting with contentment, when Bielinski came back to sit down next to us and started eating. We chewed in silence. We heard the sound the plastic tarp made as it was lifted up by the wind. There were also bird calls, some very near, on our side of the water, and others that answered distantly from the opposite riverbank. The presence of the shrill cry and its imprecise double, struggling to pierce the air, was the full scope of this landscape and the width of the river transposed into sounds, and Bielinski's wooden shack seemed even smaller within it. We were four silhouettes leaning over blue plates, four lost points that were barely visible, ready to be swept away, unmoving. Beyond the woods, the old world and the new world, the one of phantoms and the one of the living, were spinning furiously.

It was a relief when, after Bielinski had cleared the table as meticulously as he had set it, he asked my assistant with the cloves to keep an eye on Heniek, who was swaying gently, and led me farther down from the shack to the muddy riverbanks. I felt the presence of his moving body next to me. He walked with his hands in his pockets, stopped, and looked at the small islands formed in the middle of the water by patches of reeds. He grabbed a stick, pushed it into the ground, observed the hole it had made, and threw the stick back into the water, where it floated for a few moments on the surface before disappearing. He stopped and took my two hands in his.

"I have nothing to reveal to you, mademoiselle madame, nothing to leave with you, nothing to pass on. Well that's not entirely true, maybe later, a package for my friend Jan in Paris. I'll give you his address. *You* will be the one delivering something, madame mademoiselle.

"I feel good here. I walk with Heniek, we lie flat on our backs and look at the clouds. The clouds around here are Baudelaire's kind. Heniek laughs, I fall asleep with my back against the ground. We get cold, we go back to the house, and we eat some soup. Tomato, a Polish specialty. I feel good. In a manner of speaking, that is, if I want to be emphatic about it. And you like emphasis, don't you? I would say I have stopped crossing over, and now I am being crossed over. Crossed over by the water, by my halfwit son, by the seasons, by the clouds. You find this sad, but you can't imagine how good it is to give up your future. It's just wonderful. I'm serious! I'm serious!"

He laughed openly. He let go of my hands and continued walking quickly. I had to run to climb up to where he was. He turned right onto a path leading to a perfectly demarcated rectangular wood where birch trees rose up every twenty inches. I was running behind him when he stopped short. At his feet I noticed a half-buried object. Under the melted snow, a child's slipper gradually appeared, brown with dirt. The laces were still knotted. It was an old-fashioned slipper, made of leather stamped with rosette motifs. The eyelets reinforced with metal rings, which once must have been a beautiful shiny black, were now covered in rust. The slipper was resting on top of the snow, abandoned at the foot of the birch trees. Bielinski had stopped laughing and walking. He was standing still and watching me as I looked at the little shoe, unable to move.

I kept standing straight, attentive to the movements of my back and shoulders—careful not to stoop, don't break, don't give in—as I resisted the waves of anxiety coming one by one to infiltrate, invisibly and rapidly, the porous border of my skin. I started crying without realizing it, the tears flowed obligingly, effusively, my nose dripped, and I didn't have a handkerchief. The shoe, naked in its abandonment, had been fused onto the muddy earth like a seashell onto a rock, like a mineral fossil, a useless and lasting trace I didn't know how else to respond to except by crying with fear.

Bielinski took the shoe, cleaned it with his handkerchief, put it in the pocket of his coat that was too big, and took me by the hand, the way you guide a child frozen in the dark. He brought me back over by the riverbank and approached a thicket of reeds. He released my hand and pulled out a boat that had been hidden from under the green mass. I let him do this without moving. I heard, though, the sound of his breathing, and the difficulty he was having dragging the boat over to the water.

"Get in."

I almost slipped in the mud. He sat me down on one of two wooden benches. Holding the boat with one hand, he turned around toward the undergrowth to pull from it— he had suddenly become agile—a pair of oars. He sat down across from me and energetically began moving the oars in one perfectly mastered motion. Barely a few yards from the shore, the ice kept us from continuing and we started to stall between two blocks of frozen snow that stretched pale as far as we could see. It made no difference; we were already between two riverbanks, and the groups of trees running upstream and downstream into the distance wrapped them-selves around us. We could let our faces be warmed by the winter sun. The birds, hardly visible behind the reeds, were spreading their wings.

"You see, madame mademoiselle, we are in the middle of time."

I had noticed, in fact, on the map in the assistant's car, that we were less than nine miles from the small town of my father's father, his mother, and his aunt. The town in the multicolored canvases. And in the barely stirring rowboat, I remembered well the gray photo placed just next to one of

Schoenberg's paper cutters in the library. Light gray for the water, dark gray for the riverbanks, and almost black for the two triumphant silhouettes surrounded by white foam who were moving about amid the calm waves.

"Heniek's mother died years ago. She was born around here, a small town near Bug. Little Jewish girl, a child during the war. Locked up inside the ghetto of the small town with her parents and her brother. The two children had been raised by a Polish maid, a nanny. She had remained faithful to them. She'd bring them a little something to eat. There was no wall, not like in Warsaw. Simpler. One night, the mother begs her, 'Antonina, take the two children. You've fed them, you've raised them. Save them. Take them with you.' The Polish woman takes them. Two little children. She leaves with them for her parents' house in another village. She hides them, she feeds them. Now *that's* courage. If the Germans found out, she would be risking her own life and her parents' lives. A few months pass. In the village, it starts to be known about, talked about. Antonina's house. Two hidden Jewish children. The village is at risk, too. Death. Farmers come to see her, they know she's hiding little Jews. She must kill them. If she doesn't, they'll come and kill them themselves, the children along with her and her parents. In their hiding place, a nook in the attic, the children hear and understand everything. They hear Antonina speaking with her parents. She comes up to the attic and tells them they have to leave. Heniek's mother, the oldest, maybe seven, pleads with her. 'Don't kill us, Nina, don't kill us, please, we'll hide better, we'll be nice. Don't kill us.' Antonina doesn't answer and takes the two children. They leave in the night. In the distance they see the shadow of the farmers, watching. The children cry, they yell. She leads them toward the woods. She digs a hole and puts the children in it. They have to wait for her, she's going to come back, she says. The children are crying. 'Stay here, I will come back.' She leaves them a little bread, a little milk. She leaves. The children stay there, terrorized, with the bread and milk. They wait. One day, one night. Two days, two nights. Three days, four nights. On the fourth night, Antonina is there. She brings them back to the same house but to another hiding place: a hole inside the pigsty. Impossible to find. The others believed she had killed them. The kids stayed there for two years, until the end of the war. After the war, the three of them left the village. The farmers wanted gold, the Jews' gold. They were convinced that Antonina had been given some gold by Jewish parents but there was no gold, nothing. So the three of them left. The farmers killed Antonina's parents. The children's parents had been dead for a long time . . . The woods, the rivers . . . So there you go, our fairy tales."

Night had fallen and I was shivering, my feet covered by the stagnant water in the bottom of the rowboat. When we landed near the house, the assistant had put out chairs that were lying scattered on the grass. He was fussing over a pile of wood.

Excited, Heniek followed him, wielding branches which he balanced on top of the assistant's cleverly constructed pyramid. It stank of silt and cloves. Behind the house, nothing more of the forest could be seen except the harsh architecture of the trees. The assistant lit a match and all of our faces were suddenly illuminated by the orange flames climbing tall toward the sky. Sitting on the chairs next to each other, we were warmed and protected by them. We watched the insects that came to play in the sparks' shifting waves: they were lit up and then fell down to the ground, blackened and inert. Bielinski had moved Heniek's chair closer to his, and his son's head rested against him in his arms. Absorbed by the heat, freed from words, he stroked his hair, and even from a distance I could feel the unique fluid of this caress, this contact as intense as if they had been skin against skin, soul against soul. All the pain and the joy, the defeated valor, the impulses denied, and the secret fevers mingled together under the pads of Bielinski's fingers, giving life to the back-and-forth movement that was taking the necessary measurements of his son's soft-prickly hair and the heat of the skull beating under his hand.

Encouraged by the silence, the assistant comfortably began to hum, but our immobility intimidated him. He hummed softer and softer, then finally gave up and the silence returned. The sky had become black on top of the water and I could still see, above this dark bottom, the uncertain and transparent shape of sailing clouds.

So yes, I told myself, it was possible to find oneself, for a moment, in the middle of time, in the middle of the riverbanks, between the water and the fire, to be in the middle of a time that was filled, inhabited, and populated by faces and objects, and to be carried into their presence by water, fire, by love.

When we recrossed the woods that night, the assistant turned on the headlights, casting yellow patches onto the birch trunks like trail markers left by our fleeting presence. On the road from Warsaw, we passed through towns where nothing shone except the illuminated façade of a bistro.

Days later, after the filming was done, I went to the hotel reception desk and picked up the wrapped package of old journals Bielinski wanted to give to his friend Jan from Paris.

You will deliver this package, madame mademoiselle, to boulevard Voltaire, No. 102. Please. Bielinski.

2

***

I BROUGHT JAN THE package of books wrapped in newspaper.
I took boulevard Voltaire. I was unsuspicious of that gloomy
boulevard running straight from République to Nation, its
relics of political mythologies, its cafés filled with horse racing enthusiasts and Chinese wholesalers. At the end of it was
the faded building containing Jan's impersonal office.

I saw Jan coming down the hall toward me. He was
massive, so massive that when we returned to his office to
sit down, his chair resembled a child's toy. The smell of the
cigarettes Jan smoked was still on him; his two arms were
propped on his desk as he smiled. I saw Jan's ugliness. I heard
Jan saying "madame mademoiselle" to me. I learned that
Bielinski and Jan had once been constant companions, and
that they'd enjoyed walking together toward Barbès, where
Jan was working at the time. I didn't want to let myself be

taken in but, needless to say, Jan's presence wrapped around me like a terrifying and desirable wave.

Jan opened the package from Bielinski, examining the books one by one. He handled them slowly, opening the covers, brushing over the pages. He raised his head.

He held out one of the books to me. I was only able to read the name Alexander Blok on the cover; the title was in Polish. I stood up, wanting to get out of there and to leave him his book. But Jan continued holding it out to me and I had no other choice but to seize it with two hands. Already I was compelled to turn greedy. I was wearing a black sweatshirt, black pants, and black shoes: queen of the crows. I crept toward the exit. As I closed the door, I took another quick glance inside the office. He was still looking at me, smiling.

He could smile as much as he wanted to; I was under high protection.

Or so I thought.

It was only when he called me on the telephone a few weeks later, after hanging up, that I realized how much, from a place inside me—a walled-in crypt whose exact location I couldn't pinpoint—I had been waiting for that call.

I was still holding the mute receiver against my ear. There was a mirror in front of me. I blinked at the reflection. "Surprised?" But even though I stuck out my tongue and made faces, I was unable to resurrect myself as someone asexual, innocent, and free.

I was a prisoner.

We met one night in front of the Cirque d'Hiver. We walked, at a distance from each other, under the rain and then under the snow. Leaving the wide boulevards behind, we split apart the cold air. I looked like a Soviet child with my hood pulled up over my head. In a great blast of wind we climbed the steps to the summit of Montmartre. The streets were empty, the street lamps diffusing white lights.

At the top of the stairs, we walked past a sparkling Paris. I looked at Jan's profile, lit up by those distant fires. He could have been the brother-in-arms of my little tragic figures, the ones I searched for in Paris, in Prague, in Warsaw: insubmersible. In my head I toyed with the idea of flight, pursuit, hardship, and, at last, rescue.

Jan's hand had become hot in mine.

We passed black buildings that seemed to have come back, lifeless, from the depths of time. Perhaps, despite the darkened windows and the silent façades, the town really *was* inhabited? Perhaps all that was needed for its past lives to enter into me was to stop on a corner of the sidewalk, indifferent to the wind, and become stone, slate, inanimate material.

I saw Jan stretch backward like a gymnast. His body, from his extended fingers to the ends of his legs (and there were also his veins, his arteries, and his skin), was the bridge aligned between the riverbanks of time.

Jan alone was my landscape, the sentinels I'd met, the names and faces I'd imagined.

Under the snow our bodies were lukewarm against one another, resisting the cold.

My eyes were vast and we kissed.

Next we found ourselves in one, then two, then three, then ten cafés along boulevard Voltaire, all the way from place Léon Blum to boulevard Richard Lenoir. There were horse racing fan cafés, the empty cafés, the Chinese cafés, the back rooms, the *terrasses*. The waitresses who smiled at Jan, the ones who flirted with him as they leaned over too closely to serve him, a waiter with a stutter, the ones who flattered me by half-smiling, knowingly. We drank a lot; we had to drink. Entire bottles. We hid ourselves in the cafés and we drank. Inside my mouth I felt my breath turning sour, the makeup running under my eyes accentuating my dark circles because I was either laughing or crying. This boulevard Voltaire was a revelation, a dead, gray part of the city that had suddenly become its resounding heart. The front windows of the Chinese wholesalers jammed with packages badly wrapped in bubble wrap and kraft paper, their crude neon lights that were turned on even in the middle of the day, and the streets blocked by delivery trucks where the noise of horns and shouted insults climbed up from the sidewalk to envelop us like a vapor of sound: this was the backdrop for our love.

And like the waitresses who brushed against him, the shy waiters who smiled at him without knowing him, and like those other invisible and insistent people on the other end of the line who made his cell phone vibrate inside his jacket, though he never dreamed of answering it, just like them I wanted to stay close to Jan's body, to his heat, to his hands slicing through the air and grabbing the glasses on the table in front of him, his body always appearing ready to attack and to console.

I wanted to understand the details of his life, which was attached to mine as if it had been its prelude or invisible double. His parents' addresses before the war, the first name of his brother who died in 1943, what his father had done for a living. I asked, I filed, and I memorized, substituting an organized inventory for my selective memory loss.

"My brother's first name? I don't know anymore. Madame mademoiselle, please stop asking me questions and peering at me like that, analyzing me with your witch's gaze. Stop staring at me and then turning your head to snuggle up with your thoughts in your comfortable *what do you think* and your thorny impenetrable edges. 'I'm thinking, I'm evaluating.' Stick your head out a little bit over the guardrails, the machicolations, and look around you, just look. There's nothing to be afraid of. You say, 'I evaluate this, I note that, I compare, I lambast,' but life isn't like that. Madame mademoiselle, I know it all. Oh yes, it keeps you quite comfortable, you must be *quite* comfortable behind your barricades. But you know what? Your barricades aren't so fun. Air! Wind! And stop looking at me like that, like a witch, and then stop with your accumulations, the bricks in the barricades, stacking, stacking, all those old things. Wind!"

I laughed at him. I made fun of him. I was offended. It was a battle. And at night, in secret, on a map of Paris I marked down all of the cafés we'd been to so that I could superimpose this new map on top of the ones I had already put together.

After the cafés were the public gardens. Parks that were set back from the city, known only to nearby residents, with openings lost among the backyards and hidden from sight. We took refuge there as if in a kind of Eden, where adultery metamorphosed into a primitive idyll. He stretched out on a bench and placed his head within reach of my hands.

I stroked his head, not saying it but thinking, "Jan my love"—and "my love" came so easily to me, as easily as a reflex, as automatically as inhalation and exhalation of breath followed one another—"Jan my love, a long time ago, before we met on boulevard Voltaire and walked from café to café, before you made the plane trees on each side of the sidewalk shine whenever you came to meet me, both of us were—we were not born, but we were there—in the terrifying undergrowth, on the run, defeated. But you dug holes for me so I could hide in them, you pulled up roots so I could eat, and you collected water in the hollows of your hands so I could drink, for I was your brother, your sister, your daughter, your mistress. And lying next to each other we looked at the terrifying tops of the trees, the terrifying pieces of sky between the branches, the terrifying breath of leaves above us. And in those woods, day after day you saved me, and our bodies bear the trace of that rescue, Jan my love."

In the bedrooms—never the same ones, we were past shame—I would go searching over Jan's body, unearthing, seizing for myself the evidence of its heat, its root offshoots that plunged into lands of imagination. Held between his arms, contained by his thick thighs, my body—damp with secretions, examined inch by inch—entered into an unknown presence that took my breath away. This body contorted itself, shaken by dark and mysterious movements in which visions of silent incest flashed before me. Jan, my father, Jan, my brother. At the same time as he was thrusting into me, he was also dragging the shadows and dead silhouettes out of me.

The curtains were pulled shut in the middle of the day. It was artificial night and the double glazed windows muffled the sounds of the street. The silence was matte and round, like in an airtight chamber. Naked, skin trembling, I'd have to laugh more and drink more so I wouldn't feel what I recognized perfectly to be the injection of a poison into my veins. Then I'd also have to set foot in the city again, alone, and climb back up the boulevards pockmarked with blurry colored spots of green, red, and yellow.

And I, in turn, felt like a giant with heightened contours and a phosphorescent face. I had landed in the middle of the streets like a cadaver preserved in ice brittle as glass that had suddenly been unfrozen. A phenomenon of cryopreservation resurrected in the early years of the twenty-first century.

Perhaps I needed all of this cryopreservation gibberish to hide the reality of my betrayal as I climbed the boulevards and streets toward the window with the shining railing, toward the library and Daniel. To hide the pain that was contaminating our Robinson Crusoe life with the cruel and sexual wind of the world.

Jan and Bielinski had known each other years ago.

At the time, Jan had a print shop on the ground floor of a cut stone building on a street perpendicular to boulevard Barbès. He used to like walking around his machines, alone again in the darkness barely dented by the weak light filtering in from the windows overlooking the sidewalk. He'd greet the workers who arrived one by one in the budding dawn. The noise of the machines, the smell of the ink, the stained fingers, all of this was what Jan liked: the promise of a closed circuit that was productive and self-sufficient. All of the advertising agencies that emerged in those days— the years of flashy money, the debut of Mitterrand's presidency—entrusted Jan with their gleaming brochures that had been sweated over by overpaid graphic designers and editors.

Jan had clients in the fields of advertising, cinema, and design. He sometimes ventured to the luxuriant parties held at Le Palace or Le Sept. His joviality and colossal alcoholic decline, along with the mystery that emanated naturally from him, drew throngs of creative demimondes around Jan, who, in the early eighties, had found his kingdom. He adapted perfectly to the expected codes of behavior: expensive, excessive, demonstrative. But his most discriminating interlocutors could sense that behind his friendliness there was still rigidity, a secret unshakeable zone that was completely foreign to the spirit of the place, as if the orgies in which the evenings often ended were decadent and ridiculous children's games he had to endure without really taking any of it seriously. Because nothing, ever, intimidated him: he'd stay at Le Palace until the wee hours of the morning, drinking at the bar, sniffing directly off of tables, fucking quickly in dark corners, then go straight back to the print shop, change his shirt, and get to work with nothing on his face bearing witness to how he spent his nights.

Bielinski, the charismatic leader of the Polish opposition movement, had come to France under cover. In a café on rue du Faubourg-Montmartre he met Jan, who, despite Bielinski's perfect French, had identified his accent. From that day on, they never left each other's side again. Jan added the books and tracts Bielinski requested from him to the luxurious brochures made of glossy paper. He did this without a second thought, and in the middle of the night, one next to the other, without speaking, Jan and Bielinski would often arrange the freshly printed sheets together. Then they would leave to walk the streets of la Goutte-d'Or, where Jan had grown up after his father's departure from Poland. The books, precious ammunition in the democratic conspiracy, were then carried secretly to Poland by inoffensive tourist cars driven by French volunteers eager to do something heroic. Jan only made the trip once. He spent the three days in Warsaw getting drunk. Most likely in order to avoid discovering so much as a single trace of the life his parents had led there.

Then Bielinski went back to Poland.

Jan abandoned the parties. He closed the print shop and reinvented himself.

Business, import-export. It was vague, I couldn't really put my finger on it.

He saw a lot of people, that was for sure; he was permanently in meetings, and usually late to ours. I would wait. Then in the bedrooms I'd throw myself at him to hit him and beat him with both my fists, barely reaching the height of his chest. It was absurd and yet I beat him with all my strength, outraged by his failures. I didn't understand yet. I didn't understand anything! He pushed me away with a flick like an agitated insect. He held out his hand to me and picked me up when I fell to my knees, screaming.

"Get up, not on your knees. Where do you think you are? Voluntary servitude. None of that, none of that. Come on, forget it. I have stories. Great ones. Listen. Don't waste your time. Don't hit anymore. Get up. Listen."

I quickly felt that he was overdoing it. Too much wine, his voice was too loud, too many cigarettes smoked and stories told. He was overdoing it to make people believe in his presence. To make people believe he would always be there as brother Jan, father Jan, with an exterior full of benevolence and enthusiasm, a firm grip, steady on his two legs. Jan the boastful.

"Yeeeees, I understand, ab-so-lute-ly."

He cut out his words, delicately detaching and prolonging the vowels and bursting into great guffaws. He'd smile at invisible interlocutors who interrupted our *tête-à-têtes*, mirroring the intonations I imagined at the other end of the line. He was totally preoccupied with approval and understanding the most desperate of people. Not that he was naive, some Tolstoyan idealist lost in the world of business, but his vibration in unison with other people, whose psychic frequencies he detected with exceptional precision, was, at the end of the day, a method of seduction like any other. And then there was the experience of seeing him eat, listen, and embrace people, as though he were animated by an unshakeable and vital self-assurance. He was "Monsieur Jan," the man of confidences and admitted hopes, the universal savior, the axis of life around which, like wandering planets around the sun, the constellation of his friends, clients, and militants hoping to take shelter behind his thundering body turned. And Jan went along, laughing, promising, forgetting, and fleeing, absolutely, unconditionally, and magnificently. So people ran after him, tripping over themselves, looking for revenge. "Don't you remember your laugh, your promise, our hopes, don't you remember, absolutely, unconditionally, magnificently?" But Jan knew the virtues of forgetting and fleeing that allowed a person to be reborn a few miles or years away, untouched by the sadness of broken promises.

He would disappear for days. Weeks.

His life was as partitioned as a Comintern agent's, and like an agent, he had mastered perfectly the difficult art of the secret.

And I became greedy. Greedy for the hard-won hours when his body was mine. Greedy for his energy without which, from then on, the world around me—the streets I'd walked along and the books I'd read, Daniel, the man I'd loved—became colorless and mute.

Even my nights no longer belonged to me. In my sleep I drifted over monochromatic solids where the only things that stood out, like in Chinese theater, were Jan's bounding and luminous silhouette and mine always trying desperately to catch up to it.

The alternation of these appearances-disappearances that followed each other in an unpredictable rhythm threw me into the same emotional state as if he'd been holding me against him at the top of a cliff, fighting exaggeratedly against the elements to keep me from falling, only to suddenly let go of my body for no apparent reason and watch it fall into the void without the slightest movement to try and catch it. In reality I was lying prostrate on the bed, my limbs stiff just like a dead animal, trying to offset the magma on the inside with my perfect immobility. Fooling myself was one heck of a game. Maybe, I thought, if I could stay long enough without moving, every movement—the one unleashing itself inside my brain, whose materiality I perceived as though colored fluids were redrawing its circulation on an X-ray—would be abolished. Maybe then I could believe in my own death and finally escape from the spell and the pain.

The time for revolt came, too: I wanted to appropriate the power of disappearance for myself. I wanted to become an amnesiac, too. It was so simple. All I had to do was find the borders I used to have and ignore the new geographies. Parisian topography, the topography of my body.

I had to bring myself back to life from the red sofa to the library, behind the shining railing. So I disappeared. With a diligence that already signaled my failure. As I methodically drew up the list, certain neighborhoods became off limits to me. I paced the untouched streets with rage. I threw out the books and letters. I forgot the addresses and telephone numbers. I forgot the madame mademoiselle, the enormous eyes, the strong hands, the collapsed buildings in Warsaw, the ravenously smoked cigarettes.

Ah! My arrogant and conspicuous disappearances!

It was *not* so simple; everything spoke the language of addiction and memory. My body was dry, cut down like a tree on the bed, lifeless. A body from which all life had retreated. This was not words, not feelings, not love. This was physiology.

There was only the voice, and it was my lifeblood again, the lifeblood that redirected my hindered circulation. I put myself back together, an activated marionette, one leg in front of the other, and even the trees on the boulevard, disheveled with their branches still black from winter, kept me company as I went.

I found him. A new dark bedroom and Jan, stranded like a marine animal, no longer encumbered by his seductive regalia. It was when he relieved himself of that paraphernalia—when the silence finally settled, when he stopped trying

to reassure, to outdo, to support, to betray, when he let himself just breathe the smoke from his cigarette, when his body
lost its magnetic abilities—that he returned to his most fun-
damental essence, the void, the unnamed. His feet swung
gently off the edge of the bed, detached from the rest of his
body, and the crumpled sheet squeaked under the weight
of the continuous movement. His eyes remained closed,
tired from projecting strength, enthusiasm, or pleasure. I
moved my wedding ring mechanically along my finger; I
knit together a strand of hair. In the cracks of this silence,
I saw the thing that linked me to him, more firmly than his
constant tours de force, unfurling itself in front of me. In the
cracks, in the immobility, each of us had our space in the
wings without words that led us toward the place we came
from.

And so the penis that swells, the penis that penetrates,
is no longer an erotic attribute. It becomes a symbol, an
organic and mutual bond of survival.

In the middle of that peaceful capital, glorified for its
achievements in the gallant sciences raised to the status of
a fine art, in that modern country where pleasure spread
over the posters, the newspapers, and the Internet like a
tangible avatar in a society of overconsumption, Jan and I
were sharing fantasized miracles, an unpolished sexuality
without adornment or play. We were replaying the part of
those for whom the interlocking of bodies scorchingly pre-
ceded disappearance. And the cries of love were no longer

anything more than the cries of a threatened life turned into echoes.

He also says, "Air, wind! Let's forget! Let's live!" So we leave the center of the city for the steps of Paris, toward Marx-Dormoy. No one would find us among the short Indian shopkeepers, the crowd of junkies, the African families who spread out single file on the sidewalks. Jan buys me a ring at a stall laid out on a white sheet on the ground. I choose the thickest one: imitation ivory encrusted in imitation silver. It's too chunky, too wide, too big; it slides on my finger. For a laugh I argue over the price with the seller, a Pakistani man with pockmarked skin. He smiles and hands me the ring. Six black men are cooking corn cobs in six cooking pots in front of them.

We walk along the unused streets. Cranes, crumbling buildings, and vacant lots protected by gray and green metal fences. The workers in helmets yell, activating their machines that rise up like clumsy birds and cut into the sky. The teeth of mechanical diggers swallow the rubble and sand, the excavating cranes launch their sledgehammers against the stones revealing shreds of painted paper, orphaned walls made of black stone, the squealing of pulleys and sheet metal, the roar of explosions, the dust coming up in swirls. We look at everything, we listen to everything. Jan takes me by the hand and brings me under a cinder block archway that leads toward a building lost between two vacant lots. Some Chinese are gathered; a few are squatting in the courtyard looking at us anxiously, appearing slightly hostile. We can hear snippets of murmured prayers. We stay there like two travelers who have wandered astray at the ends of the earth. The Chinese start to move, pointedly showing us we are not welcome. We leave. At the end of the street, almost on the corner of the aboveground *métro*, we stop in front of a dilapidated façade on which bas-reliefs inspired by Socialist Realism are sculpted. Men in hats and thick women, scythes or hammers in hand, stalks of wheat, sickles.

A junkie in a half-torn gray coat, wide open, plows into us. He's babbling, saliva running out of one side of his mouth, his dreadlocks stiff with filth. He wants money, he can sing us a song in exchange. He starts, he jumbles it up. We stop him. A bill sneaked into his hand. He cries and pockets the bill; he tries to sing again and jumbles it up once more. The *métro* going by above us covers his voice. He gets annoyed and bangs into Jan and Jan takes him in, opening his arms, holding him against him. The junkie spits on the ground and pulls away, swearing. Against a corner of a pillar, a few brown and blonde-haired heads emerge from a pile of different colored sleeping bags. Their bodies are squeezed against each other for warmth.

Vendors try to pass us contraband cigarettes and we take them.

A man puts flashing lighters under our noses, Chinese toys. We take them.

An old Arab man bent in two holds out his hand. We give something to him.

We bury everything—the lighter, the cigarettes, and the toys—in my bag.

An overweight gypsy child turns on his scooter while staring at us, unblinkingly.

Our hands look for each other, our hands lose each other, our hands find each other, I hold myself against him, I take refuge against him, and I go blind, my head burrowed into his coat. I am blind, he brings his hand lightly up over my buttocks, against my back, and we keep going, we hobble along.

Delicately, too delicately, he removes his arm from my body, runs his hand through his hair, and detaches himself from me.

"I'm going. I have to."

"Okay."

I play the game; I'm still feeling powerful because he's here.

"I have a meeting, I have to go."

"Go, go."

"I'll call you."

He's already walking away. Up above, the aboveground *métro* is passing. The old Arab man slips over next to me. I run after Jan.

"Wait. What meeting? Please stay, stay, stay a little longer. Come on."

I cling to him, I beg, I squeeze.

"Three more minutes, I'm begging you. Three minutes. Stay."

"I have to go. I'm late. No theatrics."

"And where are you going? With who?"

"A lawyer, I have to see him. I promise I'll call you tomorrow. Cross my heart."

And he's detaching himself once again, his hand is letting me go, his body is leaving me; he disappears into the falling night. Alone! In the midst of the city and the beggars, the cheap ring on my finger I keep fiddling with. My legs become heavy, too tired to move. I squat down at the base of one of the *métro*'s steel pillars, across from the multicolored sleeping bags. There are empty bottles thrown all around, like a barricade of alcohol. The basketball players behind the fence—bands of boys, black, Arab, huge—throw a glance at me, elbowing each other, then return to their game, shouting. I put my bag under my seat, my head in my hands. When I lift it, I see a Vietnamese woman passing by, almost a dwarf, her thin gray hair sticking to her face. She walks, wrapped in a black anorak, squashed by a backpack as big as she is. She walks, looking relaxed on her voyage under the aboveground *métro*. She lightly touches the garbage, walking her hands along the surface. She picks some up and at lightning speed brings her hands behind her, opens the backpack, and crams into it what she has just found.

I feel my telephone vibrate. Jan is leaving a message, endless. I stick the telephone against my ear. I can't hear a thing with the *métro* going by, the car sirens, the shouts of the players, the monotonous chant of the beggars. I listen twenty times; twenty times I rewind the chopped message and put it together.

135

"Madame mademoiselle who is so dear to me, who I'm pulling by the hand. I'm in the *métro—uncertain breaks I can't figure out*—But open your ears wide, madame mademoiselle."

A shot into the fence, the ball bounces next to me. The giants in hoods shift around.

"The ball, m'dame, the ball, m'dame, could you throw it back?" M'dame stands up and stretches. I take the ball at my feet. I loosen my arm and my fist. Bang, I throw it back inside the court.

"Thanks m'dame, thanks m'dame." They call me back to reality; no longer a lost little abandoned girl whose hand has been let go of, but now a ridiculous m'dame, prostrate on top of her bag, always imagining an unconditional hand to hold onto her.

"Madame mademoiselle who is so dear to me, who I'm pulling by the hand. I'm in the *métro—uncertain breaks I can't figure out*—But open your ears madame mademoiselle to hear me speak. I'm murmuring for my fatigue is great."

Commotion; they've scored a basket. They jump into each other's arms, turning on themselves like overactive puppies. One of the sleepers at the pillar comes close to me. I hadn't seen him emerge from the backpacks. He doesn't even speak to me, I just feel his body in front of me. I don't lift my head. I dig into my pocket for loose change. He pockets the coins and leaves to sit down again on top of the bag, his back straight against the pillar. He is maybe thirty years old with short hair, a three-day beard, and delicate features.

He almost looks like an ancient prince, a portrait from Fayoum. He eyes me from atop his bag.

I jam the receiver against my ear.

"Open your ears, madame mademoiselle, to hear me speak. I'm murmuring for my fatigue is great. I'm old, it's very simple."

He's come out of the *métro*. I recognize the tapping of his steps, cars passing in the background.

"I'm old it's very simple. Less momentum, fewer erections, but to still love you, with your large eyes, the witch, the evil one, the plaintive one, but to still love you . . ."

I hear a blend of voices then the message abruptly breaks off. I listen, I play it back, three times, four times.

"But to still love you, with your large eyes, the witch, the evil one, the plaintive one, the large eyes, the evil one the plaintive one, the witch, the evil one, the plaintive one, but to still love you . . ." I finally recognize a woman's voice in the background yelling "Jan" before the telephone cuts out.

Well. I get up; there's no longer any question of fatigue, abandonment, or sinking. Predictable witch. I'm going to protect my property, Jan the Elder. I become a detective.

Boulevard Voltaire, No. 102. Fourth floor. Posted on the opposite sidewalk, I look at the windows that are still lit. A game of lights on the fourth floor. They're turned off, turned back on, turned off, and turned on again. I interpret, I analyze. The wholesalers close their shops and look at me strangely. It's 8:00; the door slams. His silhouette between the trees; he's limping slightly in a raincoat, a small bag in his hand. I let him go in front and set off a few yards behind him on the other side of the boulevard.

Place Léon Blum. I sneak between the people out getting some air. I pass by our cafés; he stops in front of a window and leaves again. Am I the only one who sees Jan, his mass under the raincoat, his dangling arms, his gray head? He feels his pockets, the telephone. He sits down on a bench to answer. I can only see his back. He's moving his hands, turning his head. The voice, the words, I don't even need to hear them. The voice is present, the words are present, and the missing one is sitting here, on the bench on boulevard Voltaire. He leaves again.

In this pursuit, I become clear, transparent.

I rejoice, all-powerful. I am his shadow.

He has passed rue de Charonne. He continues toward Nation. He suddenly crosses. I stop suddenly, half-hidden by a tree trunk. I laugh to myself; some detective I am. On the corner of rue des Immeubles-Industriels, he sits down in the *terrasse* of a café. My hideout is becoming hard to hold onto. I retreat. He's alone and I call him on the phone to amuse myself. I see him take out the telephone, look at it, hesitate, and pick up.

He doesn't even give me time to speak.

"I'm still at the office, I'll call you back. I love you mademoiselle madame."

I can't even respond because he has already put the telephone back in his pocket. I hide against a door. Huddled in the doorway, numb, I tremble.

I see a couple walking toward Jan. He folds up his newspaper, stands to greet them, and hugs each one. The man is short, sturdy, dressed without too much effort, and the woman has blonde hair put up in a twist. They have hardly sat down before all three of them launch into a lively conversation. Jan makes big gestures, they laugh. The woman moves sensuously on her chair and crosses her impeccable legs against the table. They toast.

The woman takes out some papers that all three of them quickly consult. Jan seems to be pointing to one sheet, one line. The man answers. They take turns signing. The man puts the papers back in his own bag, stands up, cordially shakes Jan's hand, and the woman gives a little sign with her head and stays seated. Jan signals to the server who returns with two glasses. The woman places the strands of hair back into her chignon and holds her glass against Jan's. They moisten their lips. The woman gently caresses Jan's cheek. He grabs her hand and kisses her in the hollow of her wrist. They drink again. They laugh. The woman stands up, dusting off the coat draped in swirls around her body. Jan has stood up to say goodbye to her. He towers over her because of his height and makes her laugh; she leaves, taking long strides in the direction of rue des Immeubles-Industriels.

He leaves a bill on the table and the server tells him goodbye, the tray plastered against his stomach.

Jan leaves in the direction of place de la République. He walks slowly on the sidewalk on boulevard Voltaire; he looks at the winter plane trees, their branches hung with the brown hulls of dormant fruit. I catch my breath a few yards behind him, my steps in his. The cell phone against my ear, I call him, I ring him, and he continues on. The telephone is vibrating against his chest, I know it. He is moving farther away.

He turns right onto the street that runs the length of the Saint-Ambroise church. The telephone rings. Jan is no longer answering. I see him disappear behind the church's white stones.

On my finger, I twirl my cheap ring.

Air, wind, let's forget, let's live.

3

SOMETIMES, WHEN I FOLLOWED the streets I'd known since childhood—and I don't know how suddenly it happened or if I had to call upon, more or less consciously, different layers of temporal perception inside my brain—the street I was walking on would all of a sudden become, in its proportions, colors, and geographic insertions, exactly the one I used to see when I was a child.

It was a brief but overwhelming experience in which the topographic landmarks of the past would submerge those of a different time.

There was one rather common symptom—everything appeared taller, higher, and more threatening—but the most spectacular part of this spatio-temporal fault that I was earnestly falling into was that I lost the sense of how the streets were divided up, even though it had been inscribed in me by force of habit. My sense of what connected the streets to each other, what constituted a trajectory, a path, and what fueled my construction of space and my own presence in that space—once again, not simply in terms of the scale, an unchanging principle, but also as far as my movement within that space was concerned—were all nourished by this archaic way of seeing, to the point that my sense of orientation was no longer "up to date" and no longer found itself guided by anything but my old childhood landmarks.

Once more, I saw the street and everything along it the way I saw it at the age of eight. It was like another city, familiar and yet strange. I was afraid of getting lost and losing my balance, the path, my head. I had to use all my strength—just like at the bottom of the water when you're almost out of breath, on the brink of suffocation, and you slam your heel down before coming back to the surface—to recover my adult perceptions, serene and closed down.

But it still existed within me, like a supernatural power lying in wait in a buried cavity: this subterranean topography that I could hoist to the surface of my consciousness and then plunge back into the depths whenever I liked, in a strange game of balancing where the passage from the present city to the recollected city—and this passage was as acrobatic as that of a man who throws himself from one bank to the other over a body of water that is normally impassable—did not so much reveal a nostalgia for places as it did the inerasable imprint of a state, that of the child I had been, projecting the power of love and the hope of life, of which it was the subject, over the most familiar and daily elements of its universe, like the streets, the houses, and the alleyways.

This ability to balance, my little supernatural power, the boundless belief in my vitality; I lost all of them irreversibly after Jan's disappearance.

In the silence and the covering up, I began living in a city reduced to a single dimension, the one where Jan no longer existed. My secret cities were dead.

My body was empty, a thing that moved, covered in skin, equipped with eyes that saw, hands that consoled, a mouth that spoke. But nothing else moved, not organs, not thoughts, not beats, not pulsations, not circulation. Everything inside me was empty and immobile.

In the middle of the night, I opened my eyes. The little one had woken up. She was crying. Daniel had already gotten out of bed; he had sharp ears. I took her from his arms and held her against me. Exhausted, I babbled the same melody over and over. She looked at me, curled up against my warm body, her eyes wide open. I stroked her head in a constant movement, feeling the surface of her skull with light taps that supplied blood to my whole arm. The child was there, within easy reach of my hand that passed over and over her hair, as light as threads of silk. Finally, she let go and fell asleep. I put her back into bed and lay down next to her. Lifeless.

Jan had disappeared.

I waited on the red sofa, behind the shining railing, for the day to start and then for it to end. About every six hours,

I fed the void. A bite for the child, a bite for the void. It was Daniel who grew thinner. He no longer had skin over his bones. He looked at me, worried, but didn't say anything. Maybe he cried sometimes when he thought no one could hear. I knew that when I got into bed at night, begging for sleep, fading into it, Daniel remained lying next to me, eyes open. We had wasted our treasures of understanding, our common languages. All this time we could have held one another so close, interlocking our souls so completely, but we had used it up. That language, that silent chirping, there was nothing left of it anymore, no reserves. There was no longer any word or gesture except our bodies lying down and the sound of our breaths.

We sat across from each other. For the first time in weeks, my brain started moving; everything became perfectly clear when I told him about Jan. And immediately, though I had barely spoken the words, barely aligned the sentences, the storm fell down upon us. Immediately we found ourselves as helpless as two passengers each grabbing onto a piece of the hull on a boat destroyed by the swell. Powerless, and haunted by the inevitable sinking.

At the beginning we did try grasping each other's hands, catching hold of each other, resisting. But closed inside my pain, as if inside a country with hermetic borders, I could not soften the effect of my own cruelty on Daniel. The only things that were possible: get up, sleep, eat, put one leg in front of the other. This is how we went along, week after week, month after month, each of us inside our sphere of suffering, inconsolable.

Daniel's body shrank; he was losing strength. He would walk for hours to calm his nerves.

We were hypnotized by the brutal collapse. Occasionally, but always too late, one of us would try to break the state of paralysis and, by bracing ourselves on our memories, try to resist the current of deterioration.

It was no longer as much about memory, feelings, or psychology as it was about ethology: we were like lab rats exhibiting "freezing behavior" that stand still as if frozen in place in the face of a predator's deadly threat, and within a few weeks, in our Montmartre bunker with the child who slept beside us, we had become for each other the incapacitated rat and the threatening predator.

My secret city had died, and with it all of the people like Daniel and Jan who had kept me out of evil's reach.

I no longer had the strength for anything but murmured invocations.

JAN

JAN

DANIEL

JAN

DANIEL

DANIEL

JAN
DANIEL
JAN

It wasn't as fun as Jules and Jim; the two first names suffocated in silence.

You got what you paid for, madame mademoiselle Bovary taking it one day at a time.

You, who had so perfectly waterproofed everything against the encyclopedias of misfortune.

But who ever told you that vicariously devouring disaster would protect you, huh? Who told you that? Nobody!

I for Icarus, I for idiot.

Me, little girl, miracle child, madame mademoiselle Bovary, a comforting gerontophile, a cruel and powerless rat.

It was the middle of my life's journey and my seven-league boots had transformed into boots of lead.

I found myself alone again on the ice floe.
The little *bijou* no longer had any seawalls to protect her.

Nothing flowed naturally from the source anymore.
From a living source; fluids, words, visions.

Of course I continued walking down the streets, pressing myself against the buildings. I continued feeding my child, taking the *métro*, washing myself in the morning. But the envelope had disappeared; my organs had flown away, the blood, the vessels, the arteries, the bumps, the even bulge, the tick-tock of the heart. I had become a substance that was so fine, so colorless, that at any moment it could have been carried off by the slightest breath, the most insignificant bacteria. The surveyor's friendliness had darkened; I was a wave endlessly agitated by a cold wind, so cold, against which I no longer had any protection.

Ah, look at her walk, the unconsoled, in her discovered weakness that arrives, boom, right into her head like a revelation. Ha! She thought she was so well-sheltered, burrowed behind yards and yards of high walls, she's the one who grew under the loving looks. Ha! Look at her dissolving and coming undone now that they've disappeared, now that the looks have turned away.

Princess of Aquitaine, your tower is gone, your star has died. You are no longer even dragging a body through the streets, just haphazardly molded matter.

Marianne, they say, is your name. Brown eyes, it would appear.

One night, you make a discovery. The matter has woken up, it is cut completely open to the bone, crying out, unbearable. And you talk to the matter, you console it, you make yourself into a mother for it, you reassure it. You say that the matter shouldn't be afraid of the abyss, that the matter should calm down, that there's hope and that it should fall asleep. And the matter falls asleep. It probably understood that there is no one else but you to take care of it.

But the miracle doesn't happen again. Too much effort. The matter is sucked backward, its destruction and non-advent already programmed.

Until then I had been a good little *bijou* who was very much alive, but I was almost forty years old and I wanted to die.

I had to look under the green liquid mass; I had to look under the sludge and sink down, body outstretched, and absorb the water. Let my tangled hair hang over my shoulders, let my tangled hair hang over my eyes and face.

Get used to the mass of hair, get used to the mass of water. Let myself soak, envelop, and leave on tiptoe for the water's end, toward its down-below.

Travel through the water without flapping my arms or legs.

Accept the coughing and spitting and the cold everywhere along my body.

I looked around me at the surface of the water, the bits of floating wood, and the lacy shrubs and bushes on the surrounding banks. On the other side, all the way up the hill and at regular intervals, the trees soared upward with every inch of their trunks. Their black branches, immaculate, were stretched toward the sky. They were a woeful army of comrades.

They were cold, cold, cold. I was cold, and I felt my feet going numb in the water.

The world was deserted.

All my faces had disappeared behind the tracery of trunks and branches. They were sunken, swallowed up, and my body was no longer inside my body.

It had become a naked tree, a branch.

The hills and trails were swallowed up with everything else around my living body, the one that walked in step, at a trot, or at a gallop to the beat of my heart and the blood pounding in my head. From my side of the water, I saw it in front of me: the sweep of naked trees, the sorrowful army of comrades.

It, that, I shiver against the branches raised to the sky and the earth all around and the fragile expanse of water. I, that, it moves to the middle of the water.

The sound of silence: my long breath mixed with the wind.

I remembered hills and trails, the hardness of the sun, dreamed faces that floated superimposed on the dazzling

green of meadows, brown ridges of cut lavender on the hillside, the lone horse that had turned its head to watch me
pass. I remembered the gray building façades in Paris and
my eyes glued to the rows of balustrades.

Everything had to be numbed, and the suffering reduced to
silence, in the cold water and the naked trees. I just had to
let myself drift to the middle of the water, between the two
banks.

And then I remembered the Atlantis.

We were sailing over the green water of the Dordogne in a
steep-sided valley between hills set on each of the two banks.
Daniel, the little one, and I were on the boat, squeezed in
amid the vacationers. We heard the guide's voice crackling
over the loudspeakers installed on the deck. He was com-
menting on the fauna, the flora, the construction of dams,
the efforts of the men who had tamed the river. The tourists
were in agreement, rapturous. The children were rejoicing.
In their summer clothes they jumped on top of the chairs,
ran from one end of the boat to the other, and leaned over
the steel railings under the shouts of mothers who snatched
them back, screaming. The mothers couldn't understand
that the children were intoxicated by the movement of the
boat, and that as colored spots they were the extension of the

warm air, grassy slopes, and clear sky that accompanied us on our promenade.

Like the others, the little one was frolicking. She formed alliances with children she didn't know, and all it took was a look or a hand signal to initiate a mute fraternity of corresponding laws that would appear opaque to adult sociabilities. I was sitting apart, on a wooden bench overlooking the water. I felt the sun's fire against my chest, and the humid freshness of the river on my face. The guide had been quiet for ten minutes, as if even he had been worn out by his spiel. The adults dozed; the boat kept moving.

Then the nasal voice returned, asking us to summon all of our attention to look down, very far down, under the reflections bouncing gently on top of the water. We were— and here the guide's voice became mysterious, almost intimate—on top of the ruins of a village that had been swallowed up by the water. He launched into explanations detailing the technical data retrieved by diving expeditions that had been organized over the last few years to bring some of the scattered debris back to the open air. A piece of the church bell and the blacksmith's tools were, at present, the only evidence of the village's centuries-old existence. But, he assured us, the outline of the hamlet had remained intact: the main street, church square, and side roads.

Silence had fallen over the group of passengers, and even the children stayed calmly beside their parents as if each one were trying to make out the village's unmoving presence under the smooth surface of the water. My little one was afraid; she was worried she'd see the bodies of drowned people emerge around the boat.

I scanned the water like the others and felt the presence beneath us of eroded stones, chipped low walls, waving aquatic plants, and the quick movements of fish. And in every part of my body—my hands holding Daniel's, my feet, my legs stretched out on the wooden bench, my neck and hair warmed in the sun, my gaze wandering between the water and my little one's white skin shining in the light—I discovered something like a piece that was needed to complete this landscape organized in layers from the most obvious to the most invisible, from the highest up to the deepest underwater.

These levels were not antagonistic toward one another; on the contrary, they harmonized with each other, each one extending. The swallowed ruins, hardly disturbed by the aquatic life, vibrated as we passed over them and we felt both their deterioration and their persistence under our feet. It was a joyous peace unlike any I had ever known.

But it didn't last. The guide was already racing through the list of rafting champions who, each year, achieved the precious alliance between risk and relaxation that is at the core of French natural heritage.

The children went back to their race, the adults to their chatting.

The little one climbed into my lap.

She looked at me with a determined look in her big brown eyes. She stroked my hair and took my hand. She was so slight; she was just learning how to read.

"Tell me exactly what happened to your mother during the war." I didn't know if it was a question or an encouragement. I saw the water and trees go by. I would have liked to make a detour, to remain protected in the heart of the valley, the refuge of sloping hills; I avoided her gaze. Did the curse really have to be reproduced and emerge again in the middle of summer, the most deceptive of landscapes?

But she wouldn't let me out of anything, not even the smallest detail. She had chosen the moment and she wasn't going to let it go.

Who arrested Perla?

What was it like in a concentration camp?

How long is the trip?

What does that mean exactly, a concentration camp?

How do you get lice?

How do you remove them?

What is there to eat?

Where are the dead people buried?

Did children die in the camps, too?

Why did they want children to die? She stopped and drove her eyes even deeper into mine, as if she had suddenly tasted the bitter fruit of knowledge.

Then her face lit up. She burst into laughter and pointed to a group of children behind my back who were mimicking animals and releasing ferocious cries. Suddenly she left to join them, meowing. Her movements were so sweeping, and the looks she threw me every so often were so exaggeratedly radiant, overemphasizing her confidence and joy, that I knew perfectly well—hadn't I done the same?—that they were intended to make me feel better, to convince me there was nothing here except this landscape lit by the August sun, to which we belonged just as much as the meandering river and the veiny tree trunks.

So I smiled at her tenderly because, and this was probably the most important thing, I needed to welcome her outpouring of reassurance. And I realized that in the future I would need to filter the fear and make it livable for her—the fear of the empty sky above us, the fear, too, of the bubbling and invisible matter moving beneath the surface of the rivers—just as my mother had once done for me.

This is what I suddenly remembered that night as I was entering the cold dark water.

The commitment I had made that summer day on the Dordogne; there was no way of getting out of it.

And it was the feeling of the little one's weight on my lap—the vision of her body leaning over the railing, watching for the bodies that might rise to the surface—that brought me back, shivering, coughing, and numb, onto the riverbank strewn with stones.

Io non mori' e non rimasi vivo. Neither did I die, nor did I remain alive.

Epilogue

Ventriloquisms

Io NON MORI' E non rimasi vivo.

Between death and life, between the two riverbanks, I was keeping myself in the middle.

The beams from the stone I had dug up in Warsaw and that now lay facing me, abandoned on a shelf in the library, could still reach me.

The stone was shining.

It was speaking.

Shamanic ventriloquism is a true gift.

No need for invocation.

Go, listen well, on the inside. The voices are there, in the folds.

Dragged outside, on the ground, impossible to walk, the Hungarian has soaked the bread in water, ripping off pieces, rubbing my lips. I lick the water, I swallow the bread. Not much longer, I hear him say. Everywhere, bodies, my legs stretched out in front of the block, I feel the earth under my back, my eyes point upward. The empty sky. Move my hand. First the finger, the other again, the earth, my nails. In my neck, a vein beating, *tchong tchong*. I hear *tchong tchong*, I feel it. It's beating, keeping me company. My finger, my hand, rocky earth. Warm sun face.

Shhhhhhhh the clouds. Finger ground stones dirt black fingers.

Back, ground, dirt, back mass inside weight against dirt—pain.

Clouds walking.

Maman Maman Maman I shout. It is dark and everything has turned white. She pulls my hand, quick quick quick outside. We jump up. She has Pesia's hand, too. QUICK QUICK QUICK. She yells. She is holding Pesia's hand. Quickly we climb down. Father, the train stopped before and he had already gotten off. Quick, quick, she says, Maman, and the soldiers are yelling too and I tangle up my feet and fall down but my mother pulled me, Pesia is crying and I hold on. We have to get in line like at school. Everyone is yelling and I get lost among all of the shadows and let go of my mother's hand. I turn, I can't find her. I'm crying but there is Sylvia, the one who was with us in Cafarelli, who is yelling at me and pulls on my arm and who brings me to my mother. And my mother is yelling too, Pesia is still crying. We have to move forward, the soldiers with the dogs are looking at us. There are female soldiers, too. I want to go to sleep, I'm hungry.

And I'm going to be scared, I'm going to be scared. Maman. I run behind her. She has taken Pesia in her arms. There are lots of trees and behind the trees there is water; it's round. The German lady hit Mme. Allouche on the back. Everyone left their suitcases behind.

"Quickly! Quickly!" The Germans are shouting in German. Everyone is bumping into each other. I'm out of breath, everything is going too fast, my mother is in front with Pesia, I'm afraid of losing her. I run. There are buildings. I hit a rock. It hurts. Pesia is crying in my mother's arms. It looks like we're going inside a fortress. There are walls, trees behind the walls, and in the middle there is an area with lots of long wooden houses. We run and run, one of the female soldiers yells in German, we go in. It's dark inside. There are beds placed on top of each other, a lot of beds. I can't see very well; people like skeletons without hair lift their heads, watching us pass. It smells bad like in the train car, I think I'm going to throw up. I don't throw up and my mother stops below one of the beds. We have to climb onto the bunk above her. She lifts Pesia onto it, picks me up, and puts me on it, too. There are cries everywhere. On the bed there is already a very thin woman with no hair. Her face is horrible. She looks at Pesia and me and closes her eyes. My mother climbs up and lies down. The three of us huddle together. I'm next to Pesia and the woman-skeleton. I ask my mother to go in between Pesia and me, it's not fair otherwise. I squeeze my mother but there is that woman next to me who smells so bad. I close my eyes. I itch everywhere. And then I'm cold.

The Hungarian next to me is repeating, he's repeating, "Soon, it's the end." The end? Of what? My end is here, stretched out with my back against the ground, *tchong, tssssss,* my eyes to the right, to the left, I'm looking at the end. To the left is the Hungarian's face. His eyes wide open, slitted, blue, skeleton head. The cuts on his skull, just next to me, are red and running. He's whispering in German—hear nothing, all of the noises rattling—orders, languages—French, German, Hungarian, Polish, Russian, Czech, Dutch—and people yelling, yelling while they walk, yelling while they eat, yelling as they fall down on the ground next to me. No more *kommandos,* no more work, disorder—which rots everything—bodies stacked in hills, in mountains. Soon mine for the piles. Prague, Prague, Prague, summer, office paper, official, American Express, Gare Wilson, departing trains, and in the heat the dark vaulted passage from Malostranské Náměstí to Triszte Ulice—beat, beat, the blood in my veins—close, close your eyes—turn, turn your head . . . *ano, tak, ya, yo, oui, tady, ici,* the body driven into the ground, *anotakyayoouitadyici, tchong, tchong,* bat, bat . . . *ya rozumim ano tak, los, los, los, los.*

Can't go there anymore, done going there, just dig your fingers into the ground, listen to the groaning cries, terrors. *Tchong, tchong,* bat, bat, bat . . .

The Hungarian yelled, "Ovadia," "I'm Ovadia." He picks me up, brings me into the block, and lays me down inside.

In the morning is the roll call on the Appelplatz, farther down than the block. The roll call is awful; you have to stay straight, straight, straight, up, up, for hours. The female soldiers pass, pass again, they count. There are kapos with them on every block. I'd like to sit down, I can't feel my legs anymore, my mother should let me sit down but she never wants to, she gives me a smack if I move. We're supposed to stay standing like this in the wind, in the cold. It's dark, it's morning. I try to close my eyes to sleep even though I'm standing up but the wind is too strong and I'm too cold. It climbs up along my legs, it freezes little by little and finally I become the cold. On the inside, on the outside, I am the cold, I am ice. An ice cube with eyes closed and even with my eyes closed I cry because it's just too hard and my mother hits me if I make a move and I know she's scared, that she doesn't want something to happen to me, but it's just too hard, too hard to stay like that and there are so many people, all the women with their horrible dresses. Maybe nobody would see me if I just rested for five minutes, just five minutes I promise, I promise my mother just five minutes, it's just too hard. My mother smacks me on the hand and pulls me up by my hair so I'm standing up again. She's scared and the commandant is passing with his very clean boots. I'm scared, I'm not even thinking about sitting down anymore, Pesia starts to cry, what an idiot, she's scared of the commandant, too. The commandant stops, says something in German to my mother, she says yes. She's scared. He looks at us, he looks at Pesia, who's crying. The other women look at us; there are so many of them, I'm ashamed and I'm scared. I shove Pesia the crying idiot. If my mother gets herself killed by the commandant it will be this idiot's fault and we'll be all alone here and then what are we going to do? We'll get down on the ground and die like the women from Revier. They're horrible. The kapos call them *choumkchtuk*, the *choumkchtuk*, the *bijoux*, to make fun of them. We will be *choumkchtuk* and we will never see Father, Toulouse, or the schoolteacher ever again. That will be the end.

The commandant went by, the female soldiers push us and it's the end of roll call: all of these women leaving and running into each other scares me. I'm always afraid of losing my mother. I take her hand. The others leave for work, we go back to the block. Maybe there will be some grass to pull up, little things to eat. I'm hungry. But the kapo tells us to follow her. My mother holds both of us by the hand and now there is a female soldier yelling at us. Pesia starts crying again and we have to follow the woman toward the stone buildings. She walks quickly, we run behind her and my mother caresses us at the same time. She tells me, smiling, not to be afraid, it'll be fine, she says. The soldier hits her with her baton like when we were arrested in Toulouse and my mother had knelt down screaming in front of the man in black and he had hit her with a baton and kicked her and finally we had gone downstairs and the concierge was looking at us, crying, and they had put us into that car that was black like the man's coat and we had all ended up at the Cafarelli casern with so many other people, and even then there wasn't a lot to eat and everyone was crying but in the end it was nothing compared to now, when it's so cold and we have to run behind this woman who also hits my mother. We go into the building and into a hallway. It's warm and the woman knocks on a door that opens: it's the commandant who has made us come into a big office that is quite warm and very beautiful. All three of us have our heads lowered, my mother answers in German and I'm ashamed because I know we smell bad since we can't wash and because I know there are lice on my head even if my mother removes them all day long; it's not her fault, but there are some and they might fall onto this rug and into the magnificent office of the commandant. I should tell him that, before, we used to bathe every day, we were very clean, but now we're here. It's not our fault and also it's so cold that even when my mother wants to wash me sometimes with a little water I cry and scream, the cold hurts, so she lifts my arm, pulls my hair and washes me anyway. She gets that hard look on her that is so frightening. Here, my mother doesn't have her hard look, she keeps her head lowered in her dirty dress, and all three of us have our heads lowered before the very handsome commandant and his boots which are also very beautiful. He has stopped speaking. He goes toward his desk, I watch him with my head lowered but I can still see him opening a drawer. What will I do with Pesia if he kills my mother and we become *choumkchtuk*? *Bijoux*? He comes over to us, he strokes Pesia's hair; she's so pretty, she looks just like Shirley Temple. He strokes her curls, he's not afraid of lice, and he gives my mother a rectangle wrapped in paper and she tells him "thank you" in German. She still has her head lowered and we walk out. My mother opens it. It's chocolate. She gives us some and she has some, too. It's good, it's good, it's good, and it warms me up and I let it melt in my mouth and I munch and munch on it and my mother starts to cry. Why is she crying if we got chocolate? It's the first time I've seen her cry.

My mother gives us some more chocolate and hides it. We go back to the block with the soldier who is yelling less than when we went and there is almost nobody there. All of the other women are at work in the *kommandos*. We stay inside and my mother carefully hides the chocolate. She tells us not to say anything to anyone, she pinches my finger so I don't tell anyone, not even Mme. Allouche or Sylvia because Sylvia might eat the whole thing and we have to be able to hold onto it or else we're going to die. "Do you understand?" she says to me, and I say yes. We climb back onto the *coya* and my mother searches us for lice.

The Hungarian gave me some more water. He's holding my head like a mother, making me drink in small mouthfuls. *Aylulu*, my mother would say to me, and I understood. I fell asleep but the Hungarian is speaking his language, which I can't understand at all. The Hungarian has blue slitted eyes; he doesn't have a lot of teeth, he is ghastly looking but he makes me drink water in small mouthfuls and that calms me down. My body comes back into my body, I blink my blue eyes into his blue eyes to make him understand that this water and these small mouthfuls calm me down and he smiles at me, like a mother, this Hungarian. He lies down on the bed frame next to me and turns over onto his other side to sleep. He manages to sleep despite my odor, my stinking edemas, the stinking shit all along my legs. The Hungarian is kind, like a mother.

I dream, I'm feverish, I babble incoherently, I fly above the bed frames, above the block, I take flight as skillfully as a bird, no more edemas, no more shit, only soft feathers waving, brushed by the wind. Down below people are aiming guns and setting up their shots, but who can catch me in the middle of the sky? I have keen eyes, supple feathers, and I split the air the way I learned to as a fledgling, like my bird father did before me. To escape the shouldered rifles I fly, I slide, I scoff. Acrobatics between the sky and trees. I jump the borders in the old way, the demarcation line, occupied zone, southern zone, passports, money, and no secrets for me, well-hidden, the great distributor, no one would have believed that the model employee would become a resistance smuggler. I calmed my fears as I entered the station, my face imperturbable, my trembling hands hidden in my overcoat, my impenetrable blue eyes. Greet people civilly in silence, sit down, cross my legs and watch over the folds in my pants. Out the window are fields, villages, forests.

Your land, Ovadia, your land, your valleys, your hills, the gentleness of their progression, the homes sheltered by oak trees, the houses in the villages stuck next to each other, compacted like an insect's outer shell. And most importantly, don't speak. The accent, the slight accent that would betray you. Silently hand them your papers, silently smile, silently look out the window until you dissolve into the landscape of your new land, the one of your daughters and the children of their children. France.

We're leaving, we don't know where we're going. Quickly, quickly. Get out of the block. We run with the Allouches and Sylvia. Maman is in front with Pesia. It's snowing. They make us climb into the train cars. We're stuck, the snow is melting. We rush into line. They're throwing bread. Everyone is fighting each other. Maman has caught a piece but her shirt is ripped. She splits it into six pieces. Two medium pieces for Pesia and me, a small one for her. The three others are for tonight, we're not allowed to touch them. She sits on top of them so no one takes them. She says that Sylvia steals. I don't know why she says this, I think Sylvia is nice. She makes me laugh, she sings me songs and especially my favorite one, *La Petite Hirondelle*. In school when we sang it in the yard, we'd get into two rows facing each other, hold our hands in a bridge, and each take a turn going under the bridge, and the swallow who had stolen the three bags of wheat would get three taps with the stick but nobody ever tapped hard so that the girls wouldn't get hurt. Here, the German women always have clubs and they hit, they hit even when women fall on the ground and the snow turns red with their blood. It makes me feel better to think about the song when we only pretended to hit so that people didn't get hurt.

Everyone is speaking at the same time; there are a lot of French women. Everyone is wondering where we're going. Some French women say that they're bringing us to another part of Germany because the Russians will be here soon. Others are saying we're going to be killed, others that we're going to be liberated. I don't want them to kill us because I'm so afraid of being cold like that, lying in the snow, and of everything around being red with blood. I say this to Maman, but she tells me not to listen. She covers my ears so I can't hear but that does nothing, I can still hear. I don't even cry. Not like Pesia who always has something wrong with her, she's hungry or cold or hurting, and who cries all the time because she's hungry or cold or hurting and it's true that she's little but still.

So this means my mother always takes care of her, more than she does of me, since I don't cry, so then it makes sense that I like Sylvia a lot. *She* sings me songs and so what if she steals a little bread.

The Hungarian tells me that the fever has gone, that this is good. It's true, I'm not as dizzy, I'm no longer flying.

Done being the bird. Back to being stuck on the bed frame. Exhausted, I return from a long journey.

In warm countries there are trees that search for water so eagerly that their roots, invisible to the naked eye, extend far beneath the ground. I am also searching for water and my roots, stubborn and tenacious, spread out under the block. They twist, they tangle, they upset everything in their path, stir the earth, send pebbles flying, uproot the plants and sink down far away, deep into the soil, then into the subsoil, until they touch and penetrate the bedrock. And you should see how my roots worm their way into the bedrock, how they infiltrate, mixing with the minerals, the fossils, and how they draw off the lifeblood that's taking the opposite path, climbing to the surface, making its way through the branches, the leaves, the waste, the dead bodies of animals, the dead bodies of men, all the way to the floor of the block, along the wooden mounts of the bed frames, and then spreading out over the misshapen body, my own, the lifeless body, my own, stretching out the hands, my own, supplying blood to the blue eyes, my own, Ovadia from Kz Bergen-Belsen, April 1944. My eyelids blink, my skin shivers, my penis stiffens, the wounds fester, organs working. Give me a little water, Hungarian, moisten my lips again, that I may look, that I may see, that I may stand up, that I may live.

The train stops in the middle of a forest. There is a path covered in snow going through the trees. My mother tells me we need to walk, that we have to walk, that I have to walk and be brave, that she's going to hold onto us but we must never, ever stop even if it's long, even if it's cold, it is impossible to stop or else we die. And the Germans are already yelling at us, we all go out into the snow, onto the path, and I feel like it's going too fast, that I'm never going to get there. I lose one of my shoes in the snow. I cry and my mother quickly bends down and picks it up and puts it back on for me. We can't be the last ones so she tells me to run, she carries Pesia and she pulls me by the arm. She's pulling me, she's hurting me. We're in the middle of the group. The Germans aren't speaking anymore. All of us go forward under the snow. There are birds; I hear them but most of all I hear in my head when I'm breathing and how fast my heart is beating. It's like a fog moving around in my head that's knocking. That's knocking.

I stop to hear the fog better and at the same time my mother pulls on my arm and a German hits me on the head. Not a big hit but still I almost fall down and my mother pulls me and lifts me up. I can't even walk straight because the snow is so deep and my feet are sinking into it. Then my mother repeats my name so I keep going; she's repeating it, she's carrying Pesia and she's repeating my name while she pulls my arm, Perla, Perla, Perla, Perla, Perla, Perla, Perla and on the *per* I put one foot forward and on the *la* the other one. I'm not even listening to the fog in my head anymore, just the *per* and the *la*, one foot, one foot.

The old woman I was afraid of at the camp, the one who ate in the corner of the block without looking at anyone, has

169

fallen in the snow. She's not moving anymore, but I barely have enough time to see her because my mother covered my eyes and pulled me and behind us I even hear someone hitting her. The snow must be red around her.

I'm not sure anymore how long we've been walking, and my mother puts her hands in the snow and makes it melt in my mouth and Pesia's and then she puts some on my face. It's not even cold because it's as if I've become the snow, too; cold snow that doesn't move, that doesn't move anymore, and I don't want to move anymore. That's it, it's over, even if my mother hits me, I won't keep going, I'm going to stay in the snow that is like me, I will stay cold without moving. I stop. I don't cry. I stop and sit down. That's it, I'm not going anymore. But then my mother leans over me and looks at me with her white face and her brown eyes shining in the middle. She just looks at me, she doesn't speak, she doesn't yell, she doesn't pull. There are just her two eyes, like liquid charcoal. She stops. She places Pesia, who is crying, next to her. Around us there are pine trees covered in white; in the snow there are the gray footprints of other people in front of us. They have left us behind. Pesia sits down in the snow. My mother sits down in the snow. A German woman comes toward us. Everything seems to be in slow motion and silent. Then I look at my mother, too, and our brown eyes meet. Everything is empty. We're going to die here.

Suddenly she stands up, she pulls me, she lifts me up, she takes Pesia in her arms and we run to catch up with the others. The German woman didn't hit us.

In a low voice, my mother says, "Almost there, almost there, don't worry we're almost there," and there is her hand in mine.

And I believe that we're almost there because there is no more forest and at the end there is what looks like a very big field. There are wooden barracks, barbed wire, towers, and all around are piles of naked dead bodies stacked on top of each other and even though my mother abruptly puts her hand over my eyes, I see everything.

We had arrived.

Breathe inside, suffer outside and the breath takes over what is suffering. The words remodel themselves, one after another, putting themselves nicely into single file in the folds of my brain. The brain that breathes, suffers, thinks, sees, lives. Body inert but brain in motion, and for this I praise you my creator, my God, because by your grace the possibility of prayer has been returned to me. God above blocks and bodies, above me. God without whom nothing and no one happens, God, accompany your creations, the bodies and the blocks, stretch out your strong arm and your firm hand over your servant, lying here before you on the grass, crawling on the ground like a stinking creature on the same level as the stones and insects, on the same level as the ground out of which I draw the strength to beseech you.

Pesia was at the soup. My mother had sent her. She wants me to go, too, but I don't want to. I know that Pesia gets a little more soup because she's pretty, even with the lice; everyone always says that to my mother. And then they say that she is so small. So my mother gives her the cup and she goes all by herself around the kitchen block and the women over there give her an extra ladleful in the cup. Once there was even a potato at the bottom. I know my mother would like me to go, too, but I don't have Shirley Temple hair, I'm not pretty like Pesia, nobody would give me any extra and even if my mother yells I won't go. And also, I know that when Pesia gets back with the cup, there is Sylvia next to us who is always watching us. She's lying right next to us, she's so thin but my mother says that there isn't enough soup for four. So she looks at us, thin, thin, and we move against the wall so we can't see her looking at us. My mother forbids us from looking at her.

No potato today, my mother takes the cup. We take turns passing the spoon. My mother always eats less than us. The three of us sit in a circle by the wall. It's hard not to eat it all and to give the spoon to Pesia and my mother. I force myself. I lick the spoon clean before I give it away. There is a noise behind us; Sylvia has come down from the bunk. She's so thin, you can see the lice on her body. She comes over, looking at us. She looks at the cup. She wants the soup. She doesn't speak, she just comes closer.

My mother doesn't even look at her, she keeps sucking on the spoon. Pesia has seen her. She gets up and motions the way you would to a dog, stomping her foot so Sylvia will go away. Even though she is small and very pretty, like Shirley Temple, when she moved like that, waving her hands and stomping her foot, Sylvia lowered her head and retreated like a scared animal. She climbed back onto the bunk. She continues looking at us but she no longer dares to move; she just looks at us. Pesia came and sat down again in the circle and we finished the soup. My mother didn't even raise her head.

After the soup, my mother did the lice. First Pesia, then me. And then I went outside with Pesia. Normally my mother doesn't want us to go out alone, because of all of the dead bodies in front of the block and on the pathways everywhere inside the camp. But now that we're used to it, she doesn't have to put her hands in front of our eyes anymore. At Ravensbrück they collected all of the dead people in one corner, but here, maybe because there are too many, there are dead people everywhere. They are all naked. Men, women, eyes open, mouths open, too. I'm not afraid at all anymore. I hide behind them with Pesia. Sometimes there are holes in the bodies with insects inside, black ants that come out in a line. Especially now that the snow has melted, now that it's warmer. We're even used to the smell. I know that my mother will not let us become like these dead people. Maybe Sylvia will be on one of the piles, but not us. The bodies making what look like mountains.

God, my eyes were wide open and merging with your sky, but then I turned my head and saw them hopping between the cadavers. Repulsive, skinny, they were squatting down and looking at the holes in the bodies, enjoying watching the trajectories of ants. My two daughters, so small, were chirping. I have found them in your gehenna. God, merciful artisan of their metamorphosis into minuscule she-wolves coming to sniff the smell of death. Is it possible to open my eyes wider than I've opened them now, trying to absorb the curve of their movements, the momentum of their hands and their outstretched fingers that barely touch? Merciful God who has made the spectacle of death familiar to these two children born of my seed, I give you thanks. They are going to pass close to me. I braced myself, I stretched my neck, pointing my eyes over them; I opened my mouth but nothing came out. Perla went by. She glanced at me, she saw I was moving my foot. She stopped for an instant; was that pity in her eyes? Is a little girl capable of pity? Then she left. Pesia was following her and got her legs caught on my foot. She tripped, gave me a little kick on the ankle for revenge, and then ran to catch up with Perla. And also, my revered God, what does one do with a father-body, a father-cadaver?

The Hungarian was sitting next to me. He followed them with his eyes, not knowing: those shadows had never played together in front of him on the banks of the canal du Midi, they had never hopped along the cobbled lanes of Toulouse, they had never sung the old songs of their new land for him . . . The Hungarian followed the bouncing little she-wolves with his eyes, and when they disappeared behind a block, he started to cry.

Sylvia had already died. The women had placed her on the pile in front of the block and my mother told me that it was over, that the English had arrived to liberate us. There were no more Germans, no more dogs, and we saw the English soldiers coming. They were walking slowly through the middle of the camp. They were in uniform. They looked to the right, to the left, and in front of them, at us, the cadavers. I think they were afraid. And there was silence everywhere. They hardly made a sound as they moved. Just behind them a few cars were coming, but they seemed to be rolling silently. Suddenly a woman shouted, I don't know in what language but they were not words, just a shout, and she crawled toward them. She was terrible to look at, no hair, her dress torn; her legs were no longer legs, just wires, and she fell at the feet of the first soldiers, who were afraid under their helmets. There was dust everywhere. First they didn't move, they stayed in place like statues and she kept screaming, encircling their legs with her arms that were no longer arms. And finally one of the soldiers leaned over and picked her up but his helmet fell off and the woman fell, too.

At that moment, I couldn't see anything because all of the women who could still walk, screaming and crying, started heading for the soldiers who were surrounded, swallowed up by all the women. My mother brought us with her. She wasn't crying, she wasn't screaming. She forced her way through the group of women and one of the soldiers—we could barely see his face under his helmet—took bread and sugar out of his pockets to give to us, and even though he was smiling, we could see he was afraid of us, despite the fact that

175

next to him we looked like little mice. Quickly, Pesia and I ate the bread and the sugar.

The Hungarian shakes me and I open my eyes. *They're here, they're here.*

Helmets, handkerchiefs over the face because of how bad we smelled.

They walk between the rows, looking at us, leaning over, speaking in English to each other.

They murmur quarantine, typhus.

Men lying down reach out their arms to them, smiling at them, and it's even worse when they smile with their deprived mouths. They no longer have faces, they are figurines, pieces of wood without teeth, but they still want to smile, they think they can still smile.

A man stops in front of me. I turn my head, lift my eyes, and I see him, my liberator. My eyes in his, the piece of wood looking at him. What will you say, soldier, when you return home, to your house where things remained things, animals animals, men men? Tell me, what will you say? About me, about the piece of wood with light eyes who is looking at you because you are my liberator, the one I've been waiting for, the charming soldier who is waking me up from the sleep of death.

He squats down next to me. He has a paper in his hand, he's writing.

Your name? Your name? Can you tell me your name?

My name, charming soldier, the name of the piece of wood, Ovadia, Ovadia Stern, son of Emanuel.

English soldier from the untouched lands of Dorset, charming soldier, make yourself God at my bedside and please, in large letters, write my name in the great book of life.

The people they put here in this room are those they have condemned to life, the ones who will come back. And I am among them.

I was intoxicated by the taste of the water, the texture of the bread in my mouth, gray dough, soft dough, manna from this new desert where each grain of sand is a dislocated body, because I also know—the English don't want to see it anymore, they've already seen too much—that behind the wall there are the piles, and in the piles is the Hungarian.

And God said to the Hungarian, "Hungarian, thou shalt not go over this Jordan."

Hey! Hungarian! I yell his name from the white bed. In spite of your strong hand and your powerful arm, you're lying in the pile.

What's your name? Votre nom?

Still the lists. Selection, pile, living.

Blue eyes, alive, son of Emanuel Stern, human body, Ovadia Stern.

The English want to save me. The doctor, the nurse, the uniforms and the light-colored blouses. They arrange the pillow, pull up the sheets, take turns pouring me water and giving me the manna of salvation. Little cachectic Hebrew man with bones poking out under his transparent skin, Hebrew man from the eradicated tribe who knows the price of survival.

Light eyes, parsimonious breathing, the Hungarian in the pile, and near me I saw my daughters transformed into minuscule she-wolves with sickly looking fur and crazy eyes, zigzagging between the bodies, hitting the bodies, mocking the bodies, outliving the bodies.

What will there be in Canaan?

That glorious country of after-the-war, after-the-Hungarian, after-the-piles.

To be removed completely from piles, blocks, deaths; to ingest, alive, water and manna; to push roots deep into the ground, irrigate the cachectic body, the piercing bones, the blue gaze that already is no longer fixed on anything, not the shadows in the white room, not the bowl of water or the one filled with manna; empty the cachectic body in brown and stinking waves, shit in the white bed.

The water and manna escape, probably, the open eyes of the Hungarian in the pile.

What would it cost to keep the water and the manna on the inside, to stick them to my bones, my joints, my flesh? Too late, broken shoring, the eyes that saw too much are sweeping the ceiling, no longer recognizing anything, the attentiveness of the doctor, the nurse, my hand taken in another hand, my palm squeezed by another palm.

This is how it finished and how the hills of Canaan disappeared.

And in that bed, with my dislocated body and wandering eyes, tell me, my God, am I made in your image? Am I the one who follows?

And God says to me, I hear him in my ear: "Lift up thine eyes westward and northward and southward and eastward, and behold it with thine eyes; for thou shalt not go over this Jordan."*

Am I the one who is? Will I always be the one who was?

The missing one who will lift up his eyes westward, northward, southward, and eastward and who will behold it with his eyes.

He's dead. What was his name?

Sylvia's dead! I shout. Her father hadn't reached us yet but I had recognized him; even though he was thin and wearing his striped outfit, I had recognized him: he was with us at the casern in Cafarelli and afterward in the train car. I remembered how Sylvia slept in his arms and how she had cried when he got out before and she found herself all alone in the middle of all of us. I ran toward him; he was still walking. There were fewer piles in the camp, there was sunshine and I was outside with Pesia; the two of us were playing. I saw him, I stood up, I ran and stopped right in front of him and yelled, "Sylvia's dead!" Then I smiled to tell him hello.

He stopped; he was very thin and very tall. I raised my head toward him and I could no longer see him very well because of the spots of sun over his face.

---

* Deuteronomy 3:27 King James Version

He looked at me without speaking and his eyes frightened me. But what could he do to me? I was a child.

Pesia arrived behind me; she looked at him, too, lifting her neck. She was so small and he was so tall.

Slowly he turned toward the sun and left for the woods. It seemed like he was going to collapse.

It was true, though, that Sylvia was dead.

We went back to the block and huddled together with my mother against the wall in the back on the right.

I put the blanket that one of the Englishmen had given me over my hair.

Pesia lay down between my mother's knees. She fell asleep. We no longer recognized anyone around us, the others from the convoy had disappeared. My mother tells me that the women are speaking in Czech, in Polish, in Hungarian, in Dutch, and in Yiddish. Bread and soup are being handed out. They tell us to eat slowly, not to fight each other, that there will be enough for everyone. There are still some women who steal the bread. They think that maybe we're not really liberated, and that now we can eat what we want. Some women in white are called in, nurses who look at us and touch us. A few wear handkerchiefs over their mouths. The weakest women, the ones whimpering, stretched out on the ground, are brought outside the block. We stay. We eat. I'm bored.

In Polish, in Yiddish, in French, my mother asks women she doesn't know if they have heard anything about Father, Ovadia, Ovadia Stern. The others don't answer or say no in

Polish, in Yiddish, in French. Once in a while women come and look at us, at Pesia and me. It's as if they've never seen children before. They look at us. One awful woman even wanted to stroke my hair but my mother grabbed her wrist and kept her from doing it. They look at us as if we are rare and extraordinary animals. And then they turn to sit and then they cry.

Some women started screaming. There was a man with a camera who had appeared at the entrance to the block. *Pictures, pictures.* A few women started hiding their faces; others, though, arranged their hair, if they had any, and cleaned their faces with their saliva. He left the door wide open, *light, light.* Some women started singing, others laughed. One in front of me waved her cup at the photographer. He yelled for all of us to look at him, *look at me, look at me.*

I had the blanket over my head. I didn't want to take it off, I was too afraid someone would steal it from me. With all of the noise Pesia woke up but she stayed in my mother's lap, she just turned her head.

He took a bunch of photos and then he left for the next block. These photos are strange. Who would want to see us, to look at us?

Who will look at us?